SUPPLICANT

SIERRA SIMONE

Cover Image: Regina Wamba

PROLOGUE

Four Years Ago

He's late.
(James Church Cason is never late.)
He's stuck in traffic. He's lost. Something happened.
(Nothing keeps Church from what he wants. Ever.)
He loves me. He wouldn't do this to me.
(But do I *know* that? Beyond a shadow of a doubt? Do I really know him well enough to say?)
He's not coming.
And on that point, I'm forced to finally face the truth.
He's not coming.
"Would you like to try him again?" the woman next to me asks kindly, nodding down at the phone in my hand. She's a stranger—someone employed by the church to facilitate wedding ceremonies—and her warmth and concern are blistering. I'm blistered with it. My face is hot, my eyes are seared with unshed tears, my voice is burnt and dry when I speak.

"No, thank you," I rasp. "I think—I think it won't do much good. I'm so sorry, but do you have any water?"

I hate the tenderness in her eyes when she nods, because it brings me that much closer to breaking, and I can't break. I won't. Not yet and not here. I look over at my little brother, twelve and fidgeting in his tuxedo, his blue eyes wide with worry. I offer him a wobbly smile.

"It's going to be okay," I say, reaching out to squeeze his hand. "At least no boring ceremony to sit through, hey?"

He looks like he's about to cry, and that also brings me closer to the brink, so I look away. Through the cracked door that separates the narthex from the nave.

There's only a smattering of people inside—fifteen, maybe, in a church that could seat five hundred. They're all here for me—fellow volunteers at the museum and friends from college. No family other than Jax, because our mother died a few years back and our father is a piece of shit who'd rather get stoned than do anything else.

No one is here for Church. No one. There's no sight of his parents, his brother, the niece who was supposed to be the flower girl, the sister who was supposed to do a reading. No friends. No other sharply dressed professors or sun-drenched archaeologist types.

Stupid, Charley. You've been stupid.

The vicar clears his throat and begins making his way down the aisle to me, to the great interest of the worried guests, and when he slips in through the door, he takes my hand.

"My dear," he starts, and he doesn't have to finish. He's been waiting up by the altar for almost an hour. I know what he's going to say.

"Yes," I say. "I should—I need to go."

"Of course," he says, just as kindly as the event planner had. "I'll tell the guests. Something vague, naturally."

Well, he could hardly be specific, could he? Since even *I* don't know why my wedding is missing its groom.

"Thank you," I say. My eyes are burning something fierce, and I know I only have minutes before I disintegrate. "Is there a side door I can—"

The event planner returns with a cup of water and an expression of supreme discomfort. "Ms. Tenpenny," she starts, using the water as an excuse not to meet my gaze, "there is a driver out front—your fiancé's driver."

There's a collective wince as we all think the same thing. Is someone still your fiancé after they leave you at the altar?

"Er, Mr. Cason's driver, I mean," she hurriedly revises. "He says Mr. Cason sent him to give you a ride to your home."

Church sent his driver.

On our wedding day.

To take me back to my place.

"Oh, did he?" I say. Softly.

A blunt, iron ball of anger sinks through all the hurt, through all the embarrassment and vulnerability, sinks right into the pit of my stomach. My anger will anchor me to the earth, it will keep me from floating away, and so I hold on to it with eager hands. Because Church doesn't get to have this. He doesn't get to have helping me, he doesn't get to have a *gesture*, no matter how pitifully small it is. He doesn't get to feel good about a single damn part of today, he doesn't get the satisfaction of looking back on the day he left a bride alone to be humiliated and heartbroken and think *but at least I took care of her.*

No.

He doesn't get that. Especially when it's coupled with

waving his family's obscene wealth in my face at the same time.

I take a drink of the water the planner brought and then hand it back to her. I take Jax's hand in mine and meet the vicar's concerned stare. "So is there a side door?"

IT TURNS out that I used the last of my pride on turning down the driver. I gathered my things into a holdall and left the church without bothering to change, which meant shoving my fluffy white skirt and petticoats through the narrow turnstiles at the Tube station, and having my little brother hold the train of my gown on the escalator so it wouldn't catch at the bottom. And then we rode the Tube home in silence, me trying not to cry and Jax practically vibrating with confused adolescent worry.

He was going to walk me down the aisle.

Now he's helping me jam my wedding dress in and out of Tube-car doors and turnstiles.

Of course he's worried.

What comes next? I have no idea. All my plans for the last few months started and ended with Church, with the dark-haired god in suits so crisp they made the rest of the world seem soft. Compared to those sapphire eyes and that hungry mouth, nothing else seemed to matter: not my terrible, barely there dad, not my little brother growing increasingly lost and uninterested in school, not the bills piling up on our kitchen table. With Church, I'd been able to pretend that everything would be okay, because how *wouldn't* it be okay in the arms of a man like him?

Jesus. What a fool I've been.

Not for the first time, I wish I had friends. Real friends,

not just a handful of people who know my name and vaguely wish me well.

I'd ask them if I'd been oblivious. Naïve .

After all, in what world did Charley Tenpenny—a destitute college student with an American accent—have to offer a man like him? Other than hours and hours of dark, delicious sex?

I blow out a long breath as Jax and I climb the stairs to our dank, tiny flat.

I won't think of the sex. I won't think of the way Church's fingers felt wrapped around my hips or curling inside me. I won't think of how wild those blue eyes would look when they lit on me, as if the mere sight of me turned him into an animal. *My angry god,* I'd whisper in his ear, leaning in close so he could feel my lips brush against his skin. *My temple. My Church.* And then I'd be seized and dragged to the nearest appropriate place for fucking. Sometimes even not that appropriate, because he could never wait.

You are my church, he'd growl in response as he pinned me against the first convenient surface and took me. His voice would be smoky and carnal. *You are all I see. All I pray.*

Unholy obsession. Hard sex. When he proposed, it felt like a fairy tale.

How could I have been so stupid? Men like him don't marry the girls they fuck in corners.

But then why did he buy me a ring? A dress? Why did he call me Charlotte Cason, as if I were already his wife?

The flat's door is hanging open when we reach it, and I'm jerked out of my thoughts so fast I nearly lose my breath. Dust swirls in the weak light coming in through the kitchen window, and from here I can detect the stale beer-and-cigarettes smell that suffuses our home. Our life. Our nasty, tattered life.

How did I ever think I could be Mrs. Cason?

"Charley?" Jax asks uncertainly.

Jax. You have to focus for your brother.

"Wait here, buddy," I tell him, handing him my phone. "Call 999 if I'm not back out in just a minute, okay?"

He nods, scared, and it's for his sake, all for him, that I muster up a wobbly smile and then push through the opened door, my wedding dress brushing against the old, stained carpet as I do.

"Dad?" I call out, expecting to see him asleep on the sofa or perhaps stumbling out of the back bedroom, stoned and bleary.

There's only silence.

I check the kitchen and the bathroom, then mine and Jax's room, and then his room. There's no one here. "It's okay, kiddo," I call out, and then turn back to look at Dad's room again, noticing for the first time what's missing.

His clothes. His phone charger.

The keys to the only car we have.

Dread claws its way up to my spine—dread just as terrible and carnivorous as standing in a church waiting for a groom who will never come—and I go back into my room and lift up my mattress.

My meager savings—scraped together from working at a café near my school and stuffed into a worn envelope—are gone. I don't need to look at my banking app to know that my account—shared with my dad—is cleaned out too. The shared account was the very reason I'd needed to stuff money under the bed, in case there came a month when we needed extra to cover rent or food because Dad had spent everything else on booze or bets or worse. It happened regularly enough that I never could build up a healthy reserve, but still, I'd managed to put enough under the mattress to supplement my tuition fees for next semester.

And now there won't be enough. Not for school, and maybe not for rent either, and oh God. I haven't just lost Church today, I think maybe . . .

Maybe I've lost everything.

Not just a future with him, but a future at all.

What am I going to do?

Focus. Focus for Jax.

"Is Dad gone?" Jax asks, his voice too solemn for such a sweet boy. "He . . . left?"

It's too much. I nod, my chin quavering and my throat aching, and then I sink onto my bed. The white skirts of my wedding dress rustle and fluff around me.

"Do you want a hug?" Jax asks, looking like he needs it more than me.

Openly crying now, I open my arms and draw my little brother into the world's longest, teariest hug, no longer able to stop the sobs from tearing through my body.

Tomorrow.

Tomorrow, I will be brave. Tomorrow, I will focus.

I'll unenroll from UCL, I'll quit volunteering at the British Museum because a resume for a career that needs a graduate degree to get started is now the least of my worries.

I'll get a job, or two or three. I'll find us a cheaper flat and buy us good food and make sure Jax is on time to school every day. I'll be the sister and guardian Jax deserves.

And I will never, ever forgive Church Cason.

But all of that is tomorrow, and right now it's today, and so I weep. I clutch my brother close and I let every single moment of agony rip through my chest and out of my throat. I give in to every horrible, self-hating thought I have, I curse myself for being stupid and poor and plain, and I curse Church for being perfect and cruel and wealthy enough to send a driver when he couldn't be bothered to show up himself. I cry until I'm lightheaded and swollen-eyed and exhausted. I cry a thousand tears for every second I stood alone waiting for Church and for every pound note my asshole father stole from me and for every class I won't get to take.

Tomorrow, I'll be furious. Tomorrow, I'll become the icy warrior I'll need to survive.

But today, when I cry, I cry for a broken heart.

And for a man with dark, dark blue eyes and a voice like smoke and sin.

1

Charley

Four years later

"Stop chatting and go faster on the champagne," Martin snaps as he shoves by. "They're drinking it faster than you're serving it."

"It's a gala for celebrities and society twats, what do you expect?" Twyla mutters, rolling her eyes at me and obviously not caring if he sees. She's a server with Hart Catering like me, but she's only doing it as a nights-and-weekends gig when she's not in class, and really, it's only to prove some kind of point to her parents, who are always begging to send her money. She only needs this job in an abstract sense, and so she tends to get mouthy with Martin The Boss.

Not me. As much as I'd love to give Martin a piece of my mind, I need Hart Catering because it dovetails perfectly with my days working at a supermarket—and I require both to keep paying bills.

Ergo, I keep my eyes down and my mouth shut.

Two more years. Two more years and Jax will be off to university and maybe something will change. Maybe I can go back to school. I'll be twenty-six then, it won't be *too* weird, right? The other students won't look at me like I'm pathetic? Or a pensioner? Like I've missed my chance and now I'm doomed to work at Tesco forever?

Here's the thing.

I never let myself dwell on Church and what he did to me. I never let myself admit—even in the privacy of my own mind—that I might still be in love with him. That I'm still nursing my broken heart because the broken heart is all I have left.

But sometimes—when I'm exhausted from working two full-time jobs plus parenting a hormonal teenager, when Martin is being a real dick, when the bills are piled so high I think they'll bury me—I let myself dwell on what life would have been like if Church had shown up on our wedding day. If he'd married me and then whisked me and Jax off to his Chelsea townhouse, so I'd be free from paying rent and could keep paying tuition.

If I'd graduated with the degree I wanted and was working for the museum where I'm currently passing out canapés instead.

If my days were filled with kisses like good gin—clean and cool and biting.

If my nights were filled with gasping, uncivilized fucks.

Stop. It.

That's the danger of dwelling on the future I wanted—it turns into pining for the man who took so much of it away. I make myself remember the gutting, lonely moments alone in the narthex, the slow heat of the tears when I realized he wasn't coming. When I realized that I'd been made a fool of —and worse.

When I realized I loved someone more than he loved me.

There's no word for stupidity that profound.

I pop open a bottle and start pouring, and Martin fusses off somewhere else in the back room, probably to scold someone else for being slow. Twyla snags one of the flutes I've just filled and knocks it back in one go.

"Come on," she coaxes as she sees my small smile. "Have one. Fuck knows this is the best shit we'll get to taste in a while."

I want to. I really, really want to. I want to have a glass of champagne and disappear into some of my favorite exhibits and forget—just for twenty minutes—that my life is a sleepless grind of work and debt and putting on a brave face for Jax, who needs to have as normal an upbringing as I can manage.

I stare at the bubbling flute for a moment, and then I sigh. "With my terrible luck, Martin will smell it on me."

"Ah yes," Twyla says, grabbing another flute as I open up a new bottle. "This mysterious bad luck of yours. Are you ever going to tell me about it?"

What would I even say?

It's nothing, really. Just got left at the altar by a scowling god —a god who still rules over the university department I had to leave because I was too broke. Oh, yes, he was my professor too, how thoughtful of you to ask.

It would make a great party story. If only I had time for parties.

Blocking Twyla's reach for a third flute, I slide the now-full tray onto my hand. "It's a tale for when we have something a lot stronger than champagne," I say with a forced grin, and then I push out the door and follow the faint strains of music to the Great Court and the event itself.

***

THE GALA IS in full swing now, the autumn sky just beginning to fade over the glass canopy that covers the court. The conversation and music together make for a dull, boozy roar in the echoing space.

I fix my *of course I'm happy to carry a heavy tray around* smile on my face and begin circulating through the room, unloading flutes at a rate that would horrify Martin all over again. With each step, the second-hand shoes I'm wearing pinch my toes and send pain rolling up the balls of my feet and into my heels, but still I keep the smile plastered on. Martin won't care if my feet hurt, but if there's one whiff of bad attitude among the staff, he'll unleash hell, and I can't afford hell. Not for another two years, at any rate.

I play one of my favorite games while I circulate to keep myself from focusing on my feet, where I pretend I'm David Attenborough observing the habits of rich people. Silently, I narrate all the elaborate mating and dominance rituals unfolding around me; I describe the elaborate plumage of the subjects, their bizarre status symbols and hierarchical negotiations.

It's a game I've been playing since I went through a fervent Attenborough stage after my first anthropology course at UCL, and sometimes Church and I would even play it togeth—

Nope. No Church. Just Attenborough. The one man who could never let me down.

I'm gestured over by a pale woman in a ball gown, her eyes glued to someone younger, prettier, and possibly more interesting than her, given the way the younger woman seems to be holding court in the semi-circle of people in which they are standing. The older woman's eyes never leave her rival as she efficiently plucks a glass of champagne from my tray, and the younger woman, who clearly is paying more attention than she lets on, reaches over and does the same, so that they're matching each other flute for flute like antagonistic cowboys matching each other shot for shot in an old Western film.

Here is the cold-blooded society maven forced to defend her committee territory from a young upstart. The upstart will have a name like Summer or Vervain, and the maven will make sure to say it as often as possible to highlight how ridiculous her very existence is. Both will use the champagne as a way to buy time for the next cutting remark.

I leave the maven and Summer/Vervain to move along the curve of the Reading Room wall, which is practically glowing against the darkening sky outside. I approach a group of men and women who are all dressed crisply and conservatively and arguing vehemently about the impact of the Asian markets on pharmaceutical investments.

Bankers. A totally different tribe than the maven and her rival.

I hand out flutes as I narrate—the voice in my head sounding like Attenborough's, old and wise and fond. *Jostling for status, these young and hungry creatures must always be looking for prey, even at a gala—*

My narration is interrupted by the slow fade of the music and a tide of polite applause. And then a voice I never thought I'd hear again rolls through the court, amplified by a microphone.

"Good evening," Professor Church Cason says.

Those few syllables—smoky and burned around the edges—spark fires everywhere inside me. Fires of panic and shock and sizzling lust.

I freeze next to the bankers, who take my stillness and the oncoming speech as an invitation to relieve me of the rest of my champagne.

Church continues, his voice coming from someplace I can't see, his words effortless and casual, like he's not slicing me open with every single one of them. "On behalf of the Institute of Archaeology at UCL, the Friends of the British Museum, and the Pella Group, thank you for coming here tonight to support Common Harvest. It's our hope that programs teaching students about the history of food sustainability and food culture will help shape contemporary attitudes to food and agriculture, as well as increase awareness and support of sustainable farming around the globe. We're all here because we're invested in the future of Common Harvest, this museum, and our young people. And because we like free drinks," he adds dryly. Everyone laughs, as if they didn't donate an obscene amount of money to be here. Those *free* drinks are probably worth hundreds of pounds a pop.

Tray picked clean by the banker-hyenas, I start sidling away, the Attenborough narration in my head completely silent, my own thoughts completely silent, everything gone except for Church's voice and the thud of my heart. He continues to speak as I angle away from the Reading Room to head back to where the caterers have staged. He gives some kind of introduction to tonight's big donor, and I think I'm going to make it without actually having to see him. I'll escape without having to see him in a tuxedo—not unlike what he should have been wearing that day four years ago.

But I don't make it.

There's more applause, and my new vantage means that I'm able to see the raised stage near the entrance to the Ancient Egypt exhibit. I'm able to see Church—so much of Church. So much of that thick, dark hair I used to pull on, so much of those powerful shoulders testing the seams of his tuxedo. He's turned away from me, he's shaking hands with another man who could rival Church in tuxedo-seam-testing, now he's stepping down right into the arms of—*oh*.

Oh.

A woman—tall and blond and in her thirties like him—hugs him briefly before giving him a soft kiss on the lips, a kiss which Church permits but doesn't return. She pulls back from him and gives him a happy smile, already talking, and he gives her an unreadable expression as he leads her away from the stage where the handsome donor begins his speech about his corporation and why they care about food sustainability and research. Tax write-offs, one would assume, but he can hardly admit that to a party of schmoozy do-gooders.

I don't know what line he ends up feeding the crowd, because I'm not actually listening to a word he's saying. My attention is solely on Church and his blonde.

I want to hate this woman currently lacing arms with my ex-fiancé. In fact, the hate is right there at my fingertips, burning against the cool tray and begging to be unleashed.

Hate for her. Hate for him.

Hate for this terrible, itchy white shirt that marks me as staff and not as a guest, not as someone who matters.

But even as I force myself to take a step to the side—and then another, and another, until I finally have to tear my eyes away and watch where I'm going—the Attenborough in my mind can't help but be fair to his date. As pretty and well-turned out as she is, she's clearly not a society maven or a Vervain or a banker. Like Church, her skin is the kind of half-tan that comes from a fair person spending days and weeks outside. And though she seems comfortable in her dress and heels, she's without lipstick or painted nails. She's approached even more than Church is as they step away from the stage, and her friendly demeanor and immediate engagement with everyone who comes up to her is disarming.

No, she's not a Vervain. If I had to guess, she's another archaeologist or professor. Like I should have been.

It's not her fault. None of this is her fault. I'm just jealous that she's on the receiving end of kisses and amusement. That she gets to hear that low voice in her ear when she comes.

I decide I can still hate Church though. That seems fair.

I have to go.

I can't go.

But I don't know how I'm going to make it through the rest of tonight with Church here breathing the same air as me. Leaving isn't an option—I'm not Twyla, who's only a tourist in the Land of Unpaid Bills—I actually live there and I can't risk losing a job as steady as the one I have at Hart.

But I also can't face him. I can't be close to him, I can't talk to him, I can't pretend to be okay while he plucks a champagne flute off my tray.

If he sees me and he ignores me, I'll die. If he tries to talk to me, I'll die.

If he looks at me, and in those dark blue eyes I see any combination of regret or pity or indifference—I'll die.

How the hell am I going to survive the rest of tonight?

I can't help it; I turn back around.

It's not like this is the last time I'll ever see him; if I listen to my pride or my bank account or my self-discipline, I'll be back out here with a fresh tray in just a minute anyway—although I'll definitely be avoiding him and his pretty date if I can help it.

No, this isn't about pride or holding my ground or proving something to myself. This isn't about strength. It's about one moment—just *one*, haven't I earned that much?—of weakness.

Church is turned in my direction now, listening to someone who's chattering away at his date as said date chatters back and rubs an absentminded hand up and down his arm. He's wearing the expression he wore the day we met here at this very museum—an expression like he's waiting to be intellectually and morally disappointed by the person he's listening to. His sharp-edged mouth is in a neutral line that might pull into an irritated frown at any moment, and his jaw works ever so subtly to the side, as if it's trying his patience simply to exchange the usual social mundanities. The lights have begun transitioning to muted reds and oranges as the cocktail tables are discreetly moved to the sides to allow for dancing, and even in autumnal event lighting, he is arresting.

Arresting. Not perfect. Not beautiful. The unforgiving mouth and stern features preclude beauty; the scar slashing across his cheek from a dig accident in Jordan makes him look cruel and ruthless, which he is.

I should know.

I've often wondered if there's something wrong with me, some kind of masochistic sequence in my DNA that's somehow managed to defy evolution and common sense and lead me right into the arms of a man who could eat my heart raw . . . and did.

Even now, after he cracked my soul open, poured petrol

inside, and lit me on fire, I want him. Every cruel and terrible part of him. His brilliance and his disdain and his carnality hiding underneath it all. His rough voice and midnight eyes and the way his need for me always seemed to stun him, like he hadn't planned on me but once he'd had me, there would be no getting enough, no possible satiation. I was his to consume and his hunger was infinite, like a god's.

What would Attenborough say about that, I wonder? Are there animals in the wild who willingly snuggle up to the bigger animals who want to eat them? Are there bunnies that can't help but hop after snarling foxes? Big-eyed deer that nuzzle against the throats of wolves?

No, of course not. There's only museum-loving girls who fall obliviously and deliriously in love with their brutally depraved professors.

I hate him, of course, I'll hate him forever for lying to me, for humiliating me, for shredding my heart in an unfamiliar narthex with only an event planner and my baby brother for comfort—but I could never hate him for that depravity. Or his indifference, or his arrogance. They were the things that made me fall in love with him, senseless bunny that I was, and even now as I'm watching him barely rein in his impatience with gala small talk, I can't help but fall in love with him again, just a little bit. Just with that crisp tuxedo and with the way the reddish gala lighting makes his restless gaze a deep violet hue. Just with that mouth that used to mark sin and possession all over me in between murmured lectures about ancient religion.

It's in this single moment of weakness, this one moment I've given myself in *four years* to remember how beautiful and daunting he is, that his eyes meet mine and he sees me.

He sees me.

His face goes from bored to stunned to avid to angry in the space of a heartbeat—in the space of *my* heartbeat, as my heart surges once in my chest and then begins frantically beating out a tattoo of fury and retreat. A message even my dumb bunny brain can understand.

Go.

Flee.

Before you kill him.

Church says something to his date and their conversant, and then begins pushing his way through the crowd toward me, determination carving his proud features into something equal parts sexy as hell and terrifying as fuck.

I see the moment his eyes rake over me completely, when he takes in the catering uniform and the empty tray in my hand. More shock ripples through him, followed by more determination, his mouth sharpening into a blade as he cuts toward me through the crowd.

Go, you stupid bunny, the Attenborough in my mind chides me, and I finally listen, unfreezing and darting towards the hallway, looking over my shoulder just once to see Church moving faster, walking with long, powerful strides.

"Charlotte," I see him say. Growl. I know it's a growl even though I can't hear him over the music and the hobnobbing. His dark eyebrows are pulled together and his hands are flexing at his sides, like he's itching to grab me and hoist me over his shoulder like he used to do before the wedding. I used to joke that studying primitive history had made him primitive indeed, and he'd simply smile back and dare, *but tell me you don't like it, little supplicant*, and I never could tell him that, because I did, I did like it. I liked everything we ever did together until the day I had to ride the Tube home in my wedding dress, and then I liked nothing ever again.

The truth is that I'm a mean, tired, furious bunny—a little supplicant turned apostate and unbeliever—and I'm not hiding because I'm scared. I'm running from him because if he catches me, I will kill him.

I will scratch out his eyes while reciting passages from the Egyptian Book of the Dead, I will hum Latin hymns while I bite his heart out. I don't care what kind of god he is, he is a dead god to me, and I will build a temple to bitterness out of his bones. He will be my burnt offering and I will send that smoke all the way to heaven. I will char the world with the pride he stole from me.

Stay away, Church.

Don't you dare.

I duck down the hallway, but I know Church and I know he'll follow me right back to the kitchens if he has to, and so I set my tray against the wall, accept the annoying possibility that Martin might upbraid me later, and then scurry through a narrow door that spits me back out into the Great Court. And then I jog into the exhibits, pushing past the scattered gala-goers in Egypt and Greece until I get to the empty stairs, and I can climb up to the deserted upper galleries to wait him out. There's no one up here, and my footsteps echo loudly on the wood floors as I move from Ancient Levant to Ancient Mesopotamia.

I think I lost him.

Thank God; it would be extra awkward to explain to Martin why I abandoned my champagne-slinging duties and also murdered a guest. Hart would lose its catering contract with the museum for sure, and I'd probably be fired. You know, after the trial for homicide.

I stop in front of a case displaying a cuneiform tablet, and I allow myself to breathe all the breaths I couldn't earlier. I stare blankly at my pale reflection in the glass, not bothering to absorb either the smudges under my eyes, or the tight, scraped-back ponytail I have to wear for the event, or even the clay tablet itself. I just breathe and will my heart to stop hammering against the walls of my chest.

I don't have to kill Church. I don't have to see him.

I don't have to remember all over again why I fell in love with him.

Slowly, too slowly for comfort, my pulse begins to slow and the adrenaline begins to dissolve in my blood. Exhaustion takes its place, and tears sting pointlessly at the backs of my eyes. When will it end? When will I be free? I suddenly wish I *had* left London four years ago like I made him think; I wish I'd fought harder to get Jax and me back to America so I'd never have to see or think or *feel* about Church Cason ever again.

Hot tears start rolling down my face, and I hate them, I hate the wet slide of them, I hate how I'm weak and angry and empty and it's from the mere sight of him. The mere presence of him.

Dammit.

I swipe at the tears and suck in a shuddering breath— and that's when I hear his low, furious voice.

"Hiding from me, little supplicant?"

2

Charley

Five years ago, I'd been a baby museum volunteer, tasked to shadow one of the docents giving a private tour of the Mesopotamian and Levantine galleries. Except said docent suddenly took ill—the kind of violent, stomach-cramping ill that can't be endured anywhere except on a toilet—and I was stuck giving the tour with no training and barely any detailed familiarity with the objects on display.

The added joy? The tour group was a cluster of visiting *history professors*. You know, the exact group of people who would notice I had no idea what the hell I was talking about.

But I made the most of it. We'd had a section on Mesopotamia in my Neolithic Revolution course the previous semester, and so I faked it pretty well, adding in a few jokes and dimple-buttoned smiles to make the most of my sunny Americanness. By the middle of the tour, everyone seemed charmed, except for a lone, scowling professor in the back. Church.

I found out later that he'd drawn the short straw in his

department and was tasked with babysitting the out-of-town colleagues while they were in the Big Smoke for a conference. For a reserved man like Church, not only was spending the day with a group of strangers nigh on unbearable, but subjecting him to a tour of a British Museum gallery was akin to subjecting Vermeer to a primary school art class. Church had dug things out of the ground that now resided in the museum; they'd consulted him when reworking their Religion and Belief narrative. There was nothing a second-year undergrad could tell him about the galleries that he didn't already know so well he could put the actual curators to shame.

It was near the end, when I was pleasantly bluffing my way through a description of a Babylonian tablet depicting a naked, winged goddess, when Church finally asked a question.

"Why?" he asked in his low voice.

I paused my bullshitting, my brain stuttering at the interruption. "Pardon?"

"Why," Church asked, putting a hand into the pocket of suit trousers too expensive for a professor to be wearing, "did the Babylonians do this? What was the instinct that drove them to mold Ishtar onto this tablet? Why do you think they needed to depict her—or any deity for that matter?"

It was an unfair question to ask any volunteer docent, no matter how seasoned, and the other professors seemed to know it, shifting uncomfortably and starting to make noises like they were going to answer on my behalf.

Except I found myself answering before I could think better of it. "I think that's a reductive question. Sir," I added, so I wouldn't seem too rude. But really. It was a stupid question, on top of a *mean* question, and it was clearly designed to embarrass me. It didn't matter how well this scowling jerk wore a suit or how narrow his waist seemed under all that sleek, tailored wool. Or how devastatingly sexy that scar looked running down his chiseled cheek.

Nope. Not having it. Not even from the embodiment of every dirty professor fantasy I'd ever had.

Church's lips had parted the tiniest bit at my challenge, and then he'd drawn his lower lip between his teeth for the barest instant at the word *sir*. Like hearing me say that word was enough to make him hungry and ever so slightly unsure at the same time.

I managed to drag my stare from his mouth to his eyes as I decided to say more. I wasn't a total dumbass about this shit, and also fuck him. "What comes first, deity or depiction? Depiction forces us to manifest the god into reality. Trying to diagnose the *why* of depiction misses the better question of *how*—how did these gods actually become gods? How did the Mesopotamians leapfrog from faceless pillars at Göbekli Tepe to the fully realized form of Ishtar here on this tablet?"

The other professors murmured in approval, but Church seemed to notice them not at all. He stepped forward, blue eyes alight and mouth twitching at the corner. Not quite like a smile, but like—well, like he was enjoying himself a little. I got the feeling he was surprised by this, that he was planning on being both disappointed and vindicated in his own superiority by my answer, and the fact that I hadn't just rolled over and given him an easy victory was ... pleasing.

But his intense stare and cruel mouth made it very clear that he would have a victory from me of some sort. And boy if that didn't make my lower belly flutter just the tiniest bit, if it didn't make the Attenborough in my mind notice how primed I was to receive his mating display of intellectual feathers.

"So, Charlotte," he said, reading my name off the tag pinned to my blouse.

"Charley," I corrected with my dimples out, partly to goad him (he didn't seem like the type to indulge in nicknames, not for himself and not for other people) and also partly because I wanted him to know. I wanted to hear him grate it out against my neck while he fucked me. I blushed a little at this realization, which he noticed.

The corner of his mouth twisted even more; the fox had just seen how little self-preservation this bunny actually had when it came to asshole professors.

Hell, the bunny was only just now realizing it about herself too.

"Charley," he said, letting his rough voice linger over the syllables as he watched me lick at the corner of my mouth.

"Yes?" I whispered.

"That was a very pert little answer you gave me. But you answered a question with another question, and I don't allow that."

"We're not in your classroom," I said, a bit fuzzily. His stern "see me after class, you bad girl" voice was really making it hard to think clearly. Or remember the actual tour group now ping-ponging their attention between Church and me as we talked.

"I'm not finished yet, Charlotte."

His refusal to use my nickname let me know that I was at the end of his indulgence. *Mmm, I wonder what happens at the end of his indulgence. Spankings?*

He said, "I want you to answer your own question."

My own question. Uh, what was that again?

Oh right. The *how*.

From the rapt gazes of the tour group, I knew I'd get no help from that quarter, and from an intuition that—aside from recent revelations about the state of my panties in the presence of scarred, argumentative men—never failed me, I knew I was in choppy waters now. I didn't know enough, hadn't thought enough about this to discept ancient iconography with him.

But when I looked at him again, I could see something almost *fascinated* in his expression, and I didn't want that fascination to go away. Not because I pussed out on a hard question.

"I think cultural advances drive religious advances," I hedge.

"Most people would say it's the other way around," he countered before I could finish. "Göbekli Tepe predates the agricultural revolution, suggesting that religious practices were already transitioning before the prevailing way of life changed."

I shook my head. "I think living religions respond to the time they're in, and so it's impossible to say that the complex at Göbekli Tepe meant the same thing to the people who built it as it did to the people who worshipped in it generations later. And I think the invention of cuneiform writing meant, for the first time, gods could be described in detail and these descriptions could survive and take on mimetic life. I think the invention of papyrus and paper meant these descriptions could reach people farther away than ever before. The increasing efficiency of weapons, war, and administration meant that religion was no longer localized but nationalized. Imperialized. All of these things forced deities and philosophies to evolve in complexity and depth in a way they never would have if our technology never moved beyond carving ivory or stone."

Church stared at me for a long minute after that, and then he nodded. The effect of his nod was like having him cup a hand between my legs.

"That's a good answer," he said. "You're still wrong. But it's a good answer nevertheless."

I couldn't help it, I laughed. And when I laughed, everyone else laughed too—except for Church, who was looking at my mouth like he wanted to bite it.

Everyone chimed in then, talking about whether or not it was even fair to compare a pre-pottery temple complex with the pinnacle of Babylonian cultic expression, and then I managed to move the tour on and finish it out without any more pointed questions from Professor Midnight Eyes.

And then after I walked them down to the Great Court and not-so-subtly pointed out the places where they could spend money on scones and scarves and soap shaped like mummies, Church stayed by my side as the rest dispersed to go buy mummy soaps.

"Am I correct," he said, studying my face, "in assuming you've never given that tour before?"

My cheeks burned again, but he took my hand, enveloped it in his large, strong ones. Calluses in contrast to his cool, suited demeanor stroked rough against my skin.

"You did brilliantly," he said quietly. "No other tour guide would have been able to answer me like that, not even one who's been doing this for years. You should be proud."

"Thanks?" I said hesitantly, going all fuzzy again from the touch of his skin on mine.

"Are you in school?" he asked with sudden urgency.

"University," I said. "I—um. Second year."

Relief flooded his expression, followed by something else I didn't understand. "I should go," he murmured, and to my eternal disappointment, he dropped my hand. "Good-bye, Charlotte."

***

EXCEPT IT WASN'T GOODBYE.

The next day I was shadowing yet another docent through a private tour of Ancient Greece when I became aware of a lean, suited predator stalking my steps. As the tour moved into the next room, Church cupped a hand around my elbow and led me back into the deserted Nereid Monument room.

"Come back for more clay tablet debate?" I teased, a bit breathlessly because oh my God, he was so unbearably sexy and severe. And tall. And nice-smelling—something that reminded me of incense—woody and smoky and rich. Like he really was a church, like he was a temple. A shrine to classical masculinity.

"No," he said. "I came back for you."

3

Charley

"I'm not hiding from you," I tell Church all these years later, as I spin to face him. "I'm hiding *for* you. So I don't murder you."

I expect Church to have some kind of riposte for this because he always had a riposte for everything, but instead he goes completely still, looking like someone just kicked him in the chest. Too late I remember the tears on my face, my missing piercing, the weight I've lost. The eternal bags under my eyes. I don't look like the happy, freckly coed he was going to marry once upon a time; I look like someone who works two jobs and has a full-time internship at How to Parent a Damn Teenager, Inc.

"Christ," he whispers, his eyes tracing me all over. The cheap shoes, the borrowed uniform, the blond hair scraped into a short, stubby ponytail. The fingernails ragged from tearing open boxes at the supermarket. "Little one."

Which is when I see he looks nearly as bad off as me.

His face—always rather forbidding—has grown leaner.

Harsher. His body too, which used to be gracefully clad in muscle, now seems hardened and ruthless under his tuxedo, as if he's spent the last four years trying to push-up his demons away. A permanent line has carved itself between his brows, his mouth looks like it's never known a smile, and his eyes are the bleak blue of the coldest, deepest oceans.

He looks . . . empty. Grim and hollow and past all hope.

God, what happened to him?

And why does seeing him like this hurt as much as seeing him, period?

"No," I say, to him and to my traitorous heart, taking a step to the side. Towards Ancient Levant and the staircase. Towards not-murder, and also towards not feeling all these terrible *non*-murdery feelings. Feelings like I missed him, like I want to trace the pale scar on his cheek. "Don't *little one* me. You lost that right four years ago."

He takes a step to match mine but goes no farther. He's not close enough to touch me, but he's close enough for me to see the pulse in his neck, the tic of his jaw as he works it slowly to the side.

"You said you were going back to America to live with your mother's family," he accuses softly. "I looked for you everywhere."

"Well, I lied," I say, taking another step back. The overhead gallery lights mean his long eyelashes cast shadows over his eyes, which must be why they look so haunted right now. Why he looks like he's in pain.

"Why did you lie?"

Oh fuck him. "Why did you leave me in a church, asshole?"

He takes a step closer. "I don't want to talk about it right now."

"What does it matter? It's not like I'm going to show up in your classroom and beg you to finish what you started, it's not like it can make a single bit of difference. It's *over*—"

His eyes flash at that, and suddenly he's close, too close, close enough that if he wanted, he could slide those strong, archaeologist's hands around my hips and yank me against him. Yank me up so I could wrap my legs around his waist.

Just the thought of it has heat flushing all over me, tightness twisting between my thighs.

Scared of my body's reaction to him, I stumble back and away. He lets me, but he doesn't stop prowling closer and closer, stalking me until I'm literally backed against a wall.

He stops, just out of reach, and stares at me like I'm a virgin chained to his altar.

"It's not over," he says with so much raw determination that I almost believe him.

"It is," I say, for myself as much as for him. "It is, and you're the one who ended it."

He sucks in a breath at that, closing his eyes for a single moment, before opening them again. "Why are you working here?" he asks. "You should be in a doctoral program. You should be in the field or the lab or in your own classroom. Not as a—" he makes a vague gesture at my uniform, like even the act of articulating the word *server* is beneath him.

"You gave up the right to know what I'm doing with my life at the same time you gave up the right to call me yours." I fold my arms over my chest and try to muster my best glare while my face is still wet with tears.

Tears that seem to horrify and fascinate him all at the same time. *My depraved Church, my angry god*—

No. Not my Church.

"Let me kiss you," he says abruptly.

I stare at him like he's a lunatic, and he has to be, because there's no way in hell . . .

He steps forward, close enough that our shoes bump, and I can smell him. I can smell the incense scent of him and I can count each individual eyelash fanning above his lapis-colored eyes. "No," I say, a little distractedly. "You could have had a kiss at the altar, and then every day after that. You have any idea how often I would have kissed you if I'd been your wife? You called me a supplicant before, but I would have been a zealot for you. I would have kissed your throat every morning and your feet every night, and you would have been anointed hourly by my mouth. *You* gave that up, Church, not me."

His voice is honest and bare when he answers, "Not a day goes by when I don't think about what I could have had, Charlotte. You think I didn't want your zeal? Your mouth on my throat and feet? You think I still don't want it?"

I should push back. I should say I don't care what he wanted or what he wants. But fuck if being wanted by him isn't as intoxicating as it ever was, and the admission of his desire has hot knots of excitement tying themselves in my stomach.

He nudges closer, one shiny dress shoe pressing between my feet, and his mouth now inches from mine. "Simply one kiss," he murmurs, his stare hot on my mouth. "Surely I owe you that? At the very least?"

"You owe me everything," I whisper.

His eyes darken. "I know," he says.

Needing to see something other than him so I can just *think*, I turn so that I'm facing the wall, which is stupid, because what's my plan here? To stare at the wall until he goes away? To hope that if I can't see his sculpted mouth or haunted eyes I might regain my will to murder him? Or at the very least go back downstairs to Twyla and my champagne duties?

The other reason this is a stupid plan presents itself immediately; a large hand plants itself on the wall by my head, and I feel the ghost of a warm finger trace the curve of my shoulder.

As if Church needs my mouth or even my full attention to work his god-magic on me. Fully clothed and staring at a blank wall, I'm still trembling on the edge of senselessness and all from a single brush of his finger.

"I first found you here," he says, his finger following the seam of my shirt to its collar. "In this very room. My greatest treasure, and like all great treasures, I nearly missed seeing you, buried as you were in the crush of the ordinary and the mundane." The pad of his finger—warm and rough—whispers across my nape, and a shiver skips all the way down my spine. "I nearly walked away, and if I had, some other lover would have found you and your mind, not me."

His fingers move around the edges of my hairline, and then suddenly my ponytail holder is tugged free and my hair is loose and sifting down around my shoulders. He runs his fingers through it, he massages at my scalp and rubs away the tenderness from where it's been pulling all night.

My eyes flutter closed at the pleasure, but I still manage to say, "You ended up missing me anyway. At the church, remember?"

He ignores this, still rubbing and stroking along my scalp until my toes are curling. Or they would curl if my damn shoes weren't so tight. "The night after we met, I swore to myself that I wouldn't come back. You were too young, and I'd been a churl to you. And on top of it all, I wanted to tie you to the bed and make you talk about religious iconography while I buried myself in your cunt—and never, ever have I wanted something as powerfully as I wanted that. As I wanted you."

His fingers follow the curve of my jaw until they get to my chin and then my head is tilted back to rest against his shoulder. With one hand still against the wall and his other now toying idly with the top button of my shirt, I'm enveloped in his embrace. His chest is warm against my back, even through his tuxedo, and against my skirted bottom—

I shiver again, unable to resist the urge to press against him. Just a little. Just to confirm that his erection is as thick and hard as it ever was, a beautiful, massive thing that proved Church's divinity, because no mortal could have a cock like that. It wouldn't be fair to the other men of the world.

His breath catches as I press against him, but he doesn't move otherwise, he doesn't hoist me over his shoulder to find the nearest spot to fuck me in, he doesn't shove me to my knees to fix the problem I made—all things he would have done four years ago.

He does none of this, and that's when I know I'm in real trouble. He's going to exploit that horrible, all-consuming *thing* that's always been between us. That thing when a supplicant finally finds the temple in which to prostrate herself, when a wolf finally finds a bunny that will hop after him and seek shelter between his paws. He's making me feel it all over again.

His fingers drop to my hip, now to my thigh, now to my knee.

"You have a date here tonight," I say, pointlessly.

"And?"

Typical Church answer. Asshole.

"I—I was going to murder you," I say as his fingers hook

under the hem of my skirt and trace maddening circles up my bare thigh. It's a place where I haven't been touched in years, and my body is having all kinds of wet, shivery feelings about him touching it now.

I should stop this. Yes, I should definitely stop this.

I'm going to stop it so hard.

In, like, a minute.

"You can still murder me," Church says soothingly, his fingers now stroking along the line of my panties. My head is lolling against his shoulder and my hips are pushing against his touch, trying to get his fingers to more interesting places. "I'll let you murder me all you want. But let me make you feel better first, hmm? Just rub it all better."

He emphasizes his point by sliding a single finger under the cotton and running it over the curl-covered swell he finds there.

I gasp, and in the space of that gasp, he's rucked my skirt up to my waist and slid his whole hand down the front of my panties. He cups me hard, like he used to do every chance he got before, and my body remembers. My body remembers what my mind tries so hard to forget—that this is a man I used to trust so completely, with every cell in my body, and there was a time he rewarded that trust with a breathless worship of his own. A fierce adoration and pride.

Pride.

It was always pride with us. Pride that irritated him into aggressing a poor tour guide, pride that made me fire back. Pride that kept both of us from backing down from danger when I walked into his classroom a week after the tour and realized the mysterious man I'd been fucking for the last six nights was my new professor.

"I shouldn't teach you."

"I promise to behave."

"Liar. Luckily for you, I don't trust anyone else with your education."

So we'd done it—we'd played the promising student/flinty professor game during his lectures, and then the moment we were alone, footsteps of my classmates still echoing down the hall, I'd be yanked onto his lap and bitten and licked. In between bites, he told me everything I got wrong in my last assignment. At his flat, we'd punctuate arguments about Mircea Eliade's approach to comparative religion with hard squeezes and strokes and orgasms, and I'd tell him he was wrong about human symbolic thinking in the Lower Paleolithic while he wrapped me in rope and then fucked me however he saw fit. He graded my papers while balancing his laptop on my back as I lay limp and well-used in his bed. And whenever I said something insightful in class, whenever I won an argument, whenever I hit on something clever in my papers, I was rewarded just as ferociously as when I was corrected.

No, not rewarded. *Reverenced.*

Revered and venerated and cherished.

You're going to be cleverer than me soon, he'd murmur against my skin. *You'll outshine everyone. The other professors, me, the whole world.*

It was possibly the highest praise Church could give, since he arrogantly—but also correctly—assumed he was the smartest person in every room he strode into, and so his praise and petting over my intellectual successes never felt patronizing or supercilious. Superior, yes—asking James Church Cason to be anything else would be like asking a lion to be a mouse—but superior in a way that made me into a lion too.

For all that I later resented feeling like an idiot animal of prey, until he'd left me at the altar, he made me feel brilliant and immortal. Yes, he fucked me like an altar sacrifice, refused to accept any work or thought or argument from me that wasn't the absolute best—but there was no disharmony in that, not for us. He could be reduced to cinders by my potential and then still fuck me like I was his temple prostitute, and we moved from one dynamic to the other like hopping between trenches at a dig. And like a dig, it would look like chaos to the uninitiated—simultaneously dirty and yet regulated, both inchoate and bizarrely intricate—but to us it was home.

Until our wedding day.

Remembering that now, my cheeks heat and my eyes fly open. "Fuck you," I say, right as his middle finger grazes over my clit, and then my curse turns into a low whimper.

"A fine plan," he murmurs in my ear. "Because you were always mine to fuck, sweet Charlotte, from the moment I laid eyes on you."

His finger is perfect, it's the kiss of heaven, it's big and blunt and firm, and it's right where I need it, right where it feels *so good*. Good enough to push my murdery urges to the edge of my mind, just for a moment, just for right now.

"I'm not yours," I manage. And I mostly mean it, but I can still feel his smirk curving against the shell of my ear, because he knows *mostly mean it* is a world away from *absolutely and definitely mean it*, and he won't let me forget it.

For some reason.

"Why?" I ask on a gasp—he's just slid his fingers down to toy with my vagina, to probe possessively at where he used to own me—and then I inhale again as he pushes his finger inside and sends sparks skittering everywhere across my skin.

Four years. It's been four years without being touched by this man, and it's like taking a full breath of air after a deep, dark dive. Oxygen and life flood me, my body sends *yes please yes please* chemicals swimming through my blood, and the bright, heady wash of it all makes me dizzy. I slump back against him even more as he slides out enough to tease my clit again. "Why are you doing this?"

"Because I need to," he grates out. "Because you belong to me."

His finger penetrates me again, then a second finger. They slide and curl and stroke, and my body sings at being filled by him, filled by his will and his arrogance and his hunger. The hunger that even now has him growling low in my ear as his indelible erection makes its needs known against the soft curve of my bottom.

I try valiantly for a dig, for something that would give me some control, but not enough to control to leave. I don't want to leave. I don't want to stop. I want to ride his hand and then murder him for being the most selfish man on the planet. "Doesn't your date belong to you?"

"No," he says shortly, not elaborating and his fingers not pausing in their rhythm.

"But—"

"But she's not here with me between her legs, now is she?"

"God, you're such a dick," I groan, chasing his touch with my hips so that I'm riding his hand in truth. I reach over my shoulder and behind me to fist my hand in his tuxedo jacket, the other I brace against his hard thigh for balance as I rock against his touch.

"And you're the wettest thing I've ever felt," he says. "Helpless girl, fucking my hand. Do you miss it? Me?"

"No."

"Sweet Charlotte, you can lie with your words all you want, and I'll still know the truth." His hand molds to the shape of me—his palm grinding against my clit as his fingers press and curl inside—and he buries his face in my neck. Inhales. "Who's touched this since you left me?"

"None of your fucking business," I breathe.

Oh, he doesn't like this, not at all. I can feel his body tense against mine; his hand in my skirt is merciless, determined, it will wring an orgasm from me at all costs now, simply to erase any memory that's not of him. I should hate that, I should stop it. Shove him away and tell him he doesn't get to make me come, and he doesn't get to care about the people who *do* get to make me come.

Or better yet, I could knee him in his giant dick and then go back to my job, the one I have to keep for at least two more years.

But *fuck*, he's good at this. Even angry and jealous—or maybe it's because of the anger and jealousy—his touch is sex itself. Primitive. Greedy. Unapologetic. His palm is pure rolling pressure on my clit, his fingers are long and skilled inside me, and liquid fire is pooling in my lower belly, burning at the apex of my thighs and down my quads. He's going to make me come, and there's no doubt in my mind that he thinks he's winning some crucial point here, that he's conquering, when really I still hate him and his perfect, godlike penis, and I'm one the who's winning. I'll take my orgasm, tell him to fuck off back to hell, and then walk out of here having been pleasured *and* with the upper hand.

Ha.

"Are you thinking about it?" I provoke. "Me fucking other people?"

"Yes," he says sharply. "And I'm thinking about how I'm going to fuck you in very short order, my little supplicant, and the minute I do, you'll forget about anyone else. You'll forget about anyone but me."

Memories flash—his body toiling over mine, his firm buttocks flexing and thrusting as I clutched and scratched for him to go harder and faster; his big, rough hands covering my naked tits as he bounced me on his lap like a doll. His cruel mouth between my legs, insatiable and as merciless as the rest of him, licking and sucking me as his muscled arm bunched and moved just out of view so he could masturbate while he ate me.

There was nothing like Church in the grip of an orgasm. It was like watching potency itself, and it was so erotic to see his jaw flex and his eyes hood and his stomach and thighs jerk with the force of his spend that I'd usually come again just from witnessing it.

Oh God.

I definitely miss sex with him, and I'm definitely going to come right now, and I definitely wish he was going to come too.

No. No pleasure for him. You take yours and get the fuck out.

Oh, I'm going to take mine. Any minute now, any second, so long as he keeps giving me that hand to use . . .

Church, predator that he is, scents his impending victory. "That's right," he says. "I'm going to fuck you again, Charlotte. And again and again and again, until you're too worn out to run away from me again."

"Dream—" *moan* "—on—"

"I already dream of you," he whispers. The hand that's fucking me pushes my ass tighter against his hips, and the bar of his erect cock rocks against my bottom. "Every night. I dream of the way your wet cunt tastes. Of the way it looks. Do you remember the day I came back for you? Do you remember how I ate you that night?"

"Yes," I breathe. "*Yes.*"

"I was lost then. The moment my lips brushed against

you, it was over; I was lost and you were mine. But you were mine before that, weren't you? You were mine the moment I saw you. Right here, right in this very room, I saw you. Clever and original and so kissable with that bold mouth. You laughed at me, do you remember that? Maybe that's when I knew."

I'm so close, close enough that my knees are all the way buckled and my head is thrashing on his shoulder. "Knew what?" I manage.

"That you could survive me."

That you could survive me.

But did I survive him? Could I call the last four years *surviving* when everything that made me that electric, ambitious girl four years ago was subsumed in the crush of loneliness and poverty? Were we the perfect example of why gods and mortals don't mix?

"Church . . ." It's half curse, half plea. I'm going to come harder than I have in four years, and I hate him, and I've missed him so much that I'm going to fly apart with it.

"Charlotte." He breathes me in as his touch works me over the edge and coaxes me right into sheer, filthy bliss.

Release sears me—sparkling, squeezing, hot—it starts right behind my clit and rolls everywhere: my belly, my breasts, down my thighs to my curling toes. Church makes a ragged noise into my neck as he feels my pussy clutch at him, and I know he's thinking of how it would feel around his cock. How wet and tight. How good.

The thought of his cock in me, of him spending inside of me, drives my climax higher and harder, until I'm supported completely by the hand still working my cunt and his other arm, which comes away from the wall to band across my ribs and keep me upright as I shake and shudder my way through the feeling.

It feels nothing like coming alone in my narrow bed and nothing like the few drunken orgasms I'd received from a Dutch bartender three years ago before she moved back to Maastricht and I gave up on post-Church dating altogether.

No, this is the dictionary definition of *good*, this is the kind of *good* one uses to describe sixteen-year-old scotch or a virgin dig site with bones and sherds only inches below the surface. This is the kind of good that can change your life, that can lash you to a beautiful god and lead you down the path to ruin . . .

The kind of good that not only blinds you, but binds you.

Except I'm not bound.

Church made sure of that.

What he and I had is dead, and he killed it, and it's nothing but a relic. It could be in its very own glass case in this gallery, that's how broken and inert it is.

He slides his hand free of my sex and raises it to his mouth to lick it clean, nuzzling me between tastes, as if to praise me—and God, I like it, I like it too much, it's dangerous how much his raw animalism stirs me.

I wriggle free of his hold and stumble away, my body still trembling and my cunt wet and pulsing and already aching for him *again*, the stupid thing.

"Charlotte," he warns in a low voice.

I spin around, staggering back enough to put real distance between us. He stands there looking impeccable and barely rumpled at all, as if he went for a stroll through the exhibits and didn't just finger-fuck a server to hell and back. Only his dark, hungry gaze and the fingers he's still licking clean speak to the licentious things he's just done.

"Thanks for the orgasm," I say in a shaky voice. "Now fuck off."

A slight twitch in his jaw. "No."

"I mean it, Church. You ruined us, you ruined me, you ruined everything. Now please let me live my goddamn ruined life in peace."

"And what is that life, Charlotte?" he asks, intensity burning beneath the surface of his voice. "What is this? I don't understand how my little one is here in clothes that don't fit, too pale, too tired, too thin. How could my suppli-cant, my brilliant one, end up in the shadows like this?"

Rage, white-hot and poisonous, floods my veins.

"You want answers?" I hiss. "You should have been there to ask the questions when it would have mattered."

His jaw twitches again. He knows I'm right.

"So you answer your own question, Professor Cason, because I'm not your fuckable little prodigy anymore."

"That was never how I thought—"

"I'm leaving now," I interrupt. "Going back to my *shadows*."

"Charlotte."

I glare at him as I retuck my shirt into the waist of my skirt. "Don't follow me, don't talk to me. Don't even think about me, or I'll drive my knee so far between your legs you'll have a dent in your heart, got it?"

His eyes narrow, ever so slightly—a god assessing a rebellious mortal—and then he nods, his eyes menacingly pretty.

"Good night, little supplicant," he says softly, in a voice I know means he thinks it isn't over.

But it is. It is over.

There's no unsinning those sins of his.

4

Church

There's a Ray Bradbury story about God. Well, there're several, actually, but one in particular captivated me as a child. It's called "The Man."

In the story, a rocket ship full of explorers lands on a planet, and upon landing, they learn that God has just been there. The planet's inhabitants—joyous with their newfound revelations—invite the explorers to stay, to hear what The Man has told them. All of the explorers agree, save for the captain. Bitter and blustering on about proof, he decides to chase after The Man, to follow him to the next planet and the next and the next, until he catches Him. Until he can pin Him down and look at Him with his own two eyes.

The captain is clearly the villain of the story; a man incapable of humility and incapable of faith. He believes that if God can be chased, then God can be caught. And if God can be caught, then God can fix the unhappiness inside him. And the story says that's bad for all the usual Bradbury reasons of humanity and love being more important than ambition and greed and so forth . . . but as a child, I couldn't help but empathize with the captain. Couldn't help but think I'd be climbing back into my rocket ship too, if I knew how to chase God through space.

So I grew up and taught myself how to chase God another way. Through time instead.

I became convinced that if I simply unearthed the right temple complex or cradled the right figurine in my hands, I'd finally behold the face of God. Not in an idol-worshipping sense, but in a sacred sense, a discarnate one—my mind able to brush against God's mind, if only for a second, if only for a brief moment as I dusted ochre-stained dirt from a piece of bone or stood on a wind-whipped ridge overlooking a ritual landscape.

Unlike the captain in the story, however, I was perfectly content merely to chase. To chase was also to understand in its own way, and therefore the chasing became the singular goal of my life. To dig, to study, to write. To teach, because teaching was how one was able to dig and study. My career was more than a *profession*—it was a vocation as cherished and holy to me as a priest's. It was the one thing that mattered, the only thing I held dear.

The only thing, that is, until I was manipulated into taking a group of visiting colleagues on a tour and I first laid eyes on Charlotte Tenpenny.

She was winsomely brash and happy and faking her way through that tour with adorable aplomb. She had wild, curling hair and a spray of freckles across her pale nose and rosy cheeks.

She had eyes the color of a rainy day. A nose ring and a dimple.

And most damning of all for me, a freckle on her lower lip.

I couldn't stop staring at it. Of all the depraved shit I've done, all the men and women I've fucked and wrecked, somehow that freckled lip was the single most obscene thing I'd ever seen. *She* was the single most obscene thing I'd ever seen, and nobody else around me realized it. They were fooled by her friendly accent and her cheap business-casual clothes, by her confidence and sunniness.

She played the role of cheery intern well, but I could see the truth all over her.

She needed biting. She needed licking. She needed me.

And after she snapped back at me, held her ground against my admittedly unmannerly questions? Revealed that singular mind to me? Then I knew something much worse.

I needed *her*.

I tried to fight it—I did, and I'll swear it to God Himself once I find Him—but I only lasted a day. And then I was back for her and that freckled fucking lip.

***

YES, it's as bad as you think. I did what you think I did, and I didn't do it for some hidden, noble goal. If you're looking for a reason to absolve me, you won't find it. I can't be absolved. I'm selfish, I'm vain, I chose that selfishness and vanity over Charlotte—and yet.

And yet.

The day my director presented the options to me— marry this bold, brilliant student of mine and lose everything, or break it off and keep the destiny I'd been promised —was the day my life ended. I didn't know it at the time, I didn't perceive the knife sliding cleanly between my ribs, but there it was, a blade so long and so sharp that it severed everything inside my chest, it bled me dry until I was a shell, a husk.

You could survive me. That's what I told her last night at the gala.

A pointless observation, really, because what mattered in the end was that I couldn't survive *her*. I didn't survive her. I've spent the last four years in the opposite of survival, in the land of the dead, chanting her name to myself through the fog and incense of this netherworld I created for myself.

If you marry a student—one who was your *student*, the director had said, *it's over. You may scrape by with your job, but any hope of moving up, of getting funding—gone. You know how vicious academia can be. And her? Do you think she'll ever command any respect or find a job of her own if she marries the Professor Cason? You'll kill her future in this field before it ever starts.*

He was right. If I married her, it was over, for both of us. But what I should have known was that it was over from the minute I saw her. From the first moment I beheld that freckled lip.

She'll never forgive me. And she shouldn't.

So then why did I take the trouble of interrogating her prick of a boss to find where she works during the day? Why am I here? Inside this dingy superstore listening to children cry and trolleys rattle through the aisles?

You know why.

Because last night, with my fingers inside her body and her body inside my arms, I felt alive for the first time in four years, for the first time since I let my slutty little supplicant face the worst on her own in that church.

And more importantly, she came back to life too, fucking my hand like a beautiful whore, murmuring husky threats as her body squirmed against my touch. There was no trace of the weary server then, no sign of that tearful, tired girl. She was once again my obscene little genius, my own pillar of flame.

If I had any heart in me left, it would have broken again seeing what the last four years had ground out of her, but those same years have turned me into a vessel of ashes, and so I felt only the usual bleakness, although it's worse today. Emptier and grimmer than usual.

I suppose it could be remorse?

It's not an emotion I'd particularly ascribed to my personality—I may be fascinated by religion and God, but I'm not a kind man or a warm one. I don't even know if I'm a moral one. My only compunctions about fucking Charlotte after I learned she was my student were intellectual, were concerned with the quality of education I'd be able to give someone I also needed to see tied to my bed on a regular basis. But seeing her unhappy and worn down last night . . .

That knife is moving between my ribs again as I methodically walk the aisles looking for her. I thought I'd saved both our futures by abandoning her, but last night demonstrated that I definitively hadn't saved hers. Somehow she'd gone from horizons of unbounded academic ambition to—well, whatever the hell this is. Shelving cheap food and carrying trays around and making me want to crawl to her feet the way she used to crawl to mine.

Except her crawling was bedroom play. There would be nothing playful about my crawling. Nothing sweet about a dead man begging for one last glimpse of life.

Is this remorse, then? Does it even matter?

I find her at the end of a long aisle, stocking a display of discounted biscuits, wearing a blue shirt and black pants that should look completely boring but instead draw attention to the swell of her hips and the small, pert curves of her tits. She doesn't see me yet; she's straightening up to stretch her back and bat at the stubborn curls wafting into her rain-cloud eyes, and that knife-that-could-be-remorse severs something crucial inside of me, something that had grown back since I saw her last night.

I bleed out internally all over again, I die again, I die miserably like I deserve.

What would she have looked like in her wedding dress?

What kind of rain would I have seen in those eyes as she walked down the aisle to me?

And then she sighs and looks longingly down the aisle towards the front of the store, as if hoping to see that time has raced by and her day is almost done, and I see the freckle on her lip. A teasing flaw right in the middle of that plush pink mouth, and hot, dark urges whisper through me.

I have to bite her again. I have to taste her cunt.

Just as I acknowledge these things, she sees me. Her eyes widen fractionally—surprise and longing and anger all swirling through those gray depths—and then she narrows her eyes in a such a way that makes her look like an avenging goddess. She could be Ishtar or Lillit. She could be Nemesis or Morrigan or Kali.

Fuck, she's beautiful.

It's not that I've forgotten over the past four years—on the contrary, I torture myself to visions of her perfection daily and nightly—but confronted with it in the flesh . . .

Well, it unmade me last night. It's unmaking me now.

Spots of pink glow under her freckles as she takes a step

toward me. "What are you doing here?" she demands, keeping her voice down. She casts a quick look around to make sure we're alone, which we are—mostly. Shoppers mill around us, but they're too preoccupied with squirming children or their phones to pay us any mind.

I try to think of a good answer to her question. I used to be good at answers, I used to be better at answers than almost anything else.

I'm all out of answers now; all I have are formless, urgent questions.

Find something, Church. Find something to say.

"Last night wasn't enough."

It's the wrong thing to say, and if I thought Charlotte looked furious before, it's nothing compared to now. Her cheeks are red and her chest is rising and falling fast under her shirt. "Not *enough*?" she repeats in a low, dangerous voice. "You don't get to even *think* about having more with me. Exactly who the hell do you think you are?"

The answer comes faster than any answer has in four years. "Nobody. I'm nothing and nobody, but I don't even care about the nothingness when I can see your face. I'll be nobody forever, Charlotte, if it means I can touch you again."

Her lips part and purse and part again, like she doesn't know what to say to this, and I don't blame her. What is there to say? She shouldn't let me touch her, she shouldn't let me near her. We both know what I've done. But losing her has carved me up and scraped me clean, and I'm beyond doing the right thing now, I'm beyond everything but total honesty and raw need.

Anger settles back over her face. "Do you remember what you said to me when I returned the ring?"

The invisible knife between my ribs jabs at me. "Yes."

"You said you couldn't marry me, but you wouldn't tell me why."

Because I knew it was a shitty reason even then, I want to tell her. *I couldn't bear seeing your face when I told you that I'd chosen our careers over our worship.* But I don't tell her this. Maybe I'm still a coward.

"And then you said," Charlotte continues, and there's a thickness in her voice that betrays the tears she's pushing back, "that we could still fuck. Do you know what that was like to hear? That you'd condescend to screw me, but not to marry me? For some reason you wouldn't bother to explain?"

Knife, knife, knife. Right into the heart.

"I couldn't fathom giving you up," I admit. I'm not proud of how hoarse and desperate my voice sounds, but pride was the first thing to die after I realized what I'd done to myself and to her. I drowned it in gin and hours-long runs; I strangled it nightly as I fucked my fist to memories of her. "The idea of being without you was beyond contemplation."

"But you wouldn't marry me? *After you asked me to marry you?* God, do you even hear how fucked up that sounds?"

"Yes," I say, almost angrily. "I'm well aware."

Her eyes blaze like molten silver. "And now here you are, four years later, wanting . . . what, exactly? To berate me for not surviving you? To tie me to your bed when you still won't tie me to your life?"

"Charlotte—"

"*This* is why I told you I was going back to America," she says, spinning half away from me and yanking on her ponytail in frustration. "Because if you'd found a way to say that shit to me again, if you'd shown up with this whole 'we can still be lovers' line, I would have torn out your tongue and thrown it in the river."

"Charlotte."

"And I'm better than that. I was better than being left embarrassed and hurt in a church. And I'm better than being your hookup girl now."

"*Charlotte.*"

She finally turns and looks at me, tears shimmering over her glare. My heart kicks and bleeds and aches, and my cock gives a lazy, yawning stir and starts lengthening down the leg of my trousers. Her tears always did get me hard, but to be fair, they were usually tears from a good spanking or a deep, mascara-smearing blowjob. Tears that we agreed to.

But we didn't agree to these tears, and I caused them anyway—and I'm hurting for her and hard for her and so fucking ashamed and also so fucking obsessed and there's nothing that can break this miserable, muddy tide between us, nothing that can ease her tears and my hunger for her at the same time. Nothing that can make me deserve her and nothing that can make me stop wanting to deserve her.

I take her hand and pull, and she's off-kilter enough that she lets me, she lets me drag her back to the hallway that leads to the break room and staff toilet, and it isn't until I've pulled her into an empty manager's office that the murder threats start coming.

"I'm going to kill you," she says. "Let go of my hand so I can kill you."

I kick the door shut and let go of her hand—so I can plant my own hands against the wall on either side of her head. "Twenty minutes," I say. "I need twenty minutes."

She glares at me. "Twenty minutes before I kill you?"

Four years ago, I would have spun her around and seared her bottom pink with my palm for a comment like that. But I'm immediately and painfully distracted by the track of a lingering tear on her face as it rolls down her cheek to the corner of her mouth.

And then onto that goddamned freckled lip.

With a growl, I'm on her, I'm against her, I'm biting and sucking on that lip—my entire world the taste of her tears and her mouth—and she doesn't murder me even in the slightest. The minute I kiss her, her hands weave through my hair and tighten, not trying to pull me away, but keeping me close. Her hips begin rocking mindlessly against mine and she pants into my mouth whenever we separate long enough to suck in a breath.

"*Shit*," she hisses, and I know she's furious with herself. But even in her fury, she can't stop grinding her needy cunt against my clothed erection. It swells to full hardness to meet her. "*Fuck*."

"Twenty minutes," I demand in between bites. "Give me twenty minutes with you."

"And just what do you think you'll accomplish in twenty minutes?" she gasps out, hands sliding beneath my coat and sweater to tug at the buttons of the Oxford shirt I wear underneath it all. She's always been a glutton for my body. Matched only by my terminal gluttony for hers.

"Orgasms," I promise, moving to her neck and sucking the skin there until she groans. "One for every year we've been apart."

Her hands are under my shirt now, running up and down my abdomen with greedy caresses. The caresses are awkward because our lower halves are still grinding and mashing together, but she keeps rubbing her sex against me anyway, arching her back to get a better angle against my cock.

"You," she pants, "don't get"—*pant pant*—"to just come here"—*pant*—"and fuck me with your giant penis."

I move my mouth to her ear and feel how she shudders with the tiniest licks, the smallest of nips. "Who said anything about that? I'm going to lick those orgasms out of you. I'm going to kiss them right out of your little pussy. I'm going to fuck you with my mouth, and you're going to be so soft and swollen and hungry for more after that you're going to give me what I really want."

I pull back so I can look into her eyes—silver and glistening even in the cloudy light coming in through the office window—and so I see how they war between wary and aroused. "And what do you really want?" she asks. Her hands are roaming down to my arse now, like she can't help herself even when she's supposed to be negotiating—or murdering me, according to her.

"To be your temple again."

I think the noise she makes was meant to be a scoff, but it comes out like a choked sob. "You'll never get that back from me."

I know that. I know that like I know the feel of my own palm around my cock. But it's gutting to hear her say it aloud, and I press my face back into her neck so she doesn't see how she's hurt me.

Her hands move back up to my chest, then my shoulders, then my hair, and I think *this is it*, this is the moment she's going to push me away, and I won't get to taste her, I won't get to pour every hour of my emptiness and misery into the kinds of intimate kisses that I would rip my soul out to give her. I breathe in the sweet, soap-smelling warmth of her neck, I tell myself to enjoy this last moment of her body against mine, her hands in my hair, and I brace myself for the rejection I've earned. The rejection I deserve.

It doesn't come.

Instead, she pushes my head down—down, down,

down, until I'm kneeling at her feet. "Four orgasms," she says as she pushes me down her body. "Four and I might consider not tearing your throat out with my teeth. And you only have fifteen minutes."

I peer up at her like she's a goddess who's just spared my life, and I don't miss the tremble in her chin as she looks back down at me. Nor do I miss the flush on her neck or the hard nipples pressing against her shirt. She hates me and wants me all at the same time, and I can't blame her, because I hate myself and want her all at the same time too. Want her so much that atonement and morality are nothing right now, they are non-concepts, they can't exist when heaven itself is a mere few inches away from my lips.

No, I have to taste her. I have to lick her and bite her and scent her and mark her and remember. Remember this holy ritual we used to act out faithfully every chance we got— sometimes in bed, sometimes with her cuffed and spread for me, sometimes in my office at the university—this sacred act where I drank of her like communion wine. Where I breathed her in like the divine air of Delphi. She called me her angry god, and I was, I was her jealous, fierce, imperfect god, but we'd both known the truth. We both knew who actually worshipped whom.

She was my wind-whipped ridge over the temple complex, she was my precious artifact. When I held her close, I held God close, when I was with her, God was with me. Experiencing her is experiencing everything I've spent my life chasing after, just like the captain in the story.

My little supplicant, I think wildly, pressing my mouth to the apex of her thighs and kissing her fabric-covered cunt. *My little one. How I need you.*

I don't give her a chance to rethink this; I can't. I reach for the button of her pants and unfasten them, tugging them around her hips and bottom to her knees and then I bury my face against her white cotton knickers. I inhale her, shoving my nose into her body and making her gasp with the coarse animality of it. The minute her scent kicks into my nostrils, my cock responds with a jerking leap in the leg of my trousers, wanting out to play.

"I smell you," I murmur, angling so that I can bite gently at the cotton-covered folds. "I know you've been needing this. I know you've been thinking of me and how good it felt to fuck my hand last night."

She shudders, her fingers tightening in my hair.

"You've always liked it a little wrong, Charlotte. A little bad. And you need it so often, my sweetheart. I've never met anyone who needs release as much as you."

She shivers again, whimpering as I give her mound a final kiss over the cotton and then begin tugging her knickers down to reveal her gold-covered cunt. My own sweet chalice, my own reliquary. Gilded and gorgeous and protecting the real gift inside.

I kiss her as reverently as a priest kisses his stole, soft kisses along her silky curls until I get to her clit, which is plump and swollen, and sweet as any berry, a little fruit waiting to be plucked. I kiss it too, relishing her small jump as I do, and then I tease at it with the tip of my tongue, finally, *finally* tasting her. The unique, intimate taste that's sweet and earthy and so goddamn addictive that I've been starving for it since before our ill-fated wedding day four years ago. And the moment it hits my tongue, I need more, I need so much more and I use my thumbs to spread her apart so I can lick deeper, farther, I need it to be the only thing I taste for the rest of my life.

She gives a cry and slumps back against the wall.

"Everything," I breathe into her, barely able to stop

myself from tasting her long enough to speak, "this is everything. *Fuck*."

And after that, I can't speak. Me, the teacher. Me, the writer. And all my words are gone, totally subsumed. Burned away in the face of my need to drink her down, to mark every hidden corner of her with my kiss, and have her break apart against my lips. I keep her spread with one hand and then use the other to push her pants and knickers down to her ankles, enough to free one leg, which I sling over my shoulder. God, yes, *this*—this right here, with her thigh warming my ear and her hips angled just right against my face—I have to live the rest of my life like this. My face buried in her and my nose bumping her clit as I fuck her with my tongue, as I stab into her and swirl and lick, and then move up to suckle at her while her pleasure slicks all over my face.

"Church, you—I wanted this—so much—" Her words are barely there, just mindless pleasure words wrung from the circumstances, but I steal them for my jealous, bleeding heart anyway, I tuck them against the wounds there like bandages.

"You're so soft," I growl into her, before shoving my whole face back in again like a fucking animal. "You're so soft and you're about to get even softer, aren't you? About to make this place all swollen and slick for me?"

"I—" She can't finish. But she doesn't need to—a long, lingering suck on her clit sends her over the edge and she starts riding my mouth like she paid for it. I groan into her as she comes, as spots dance before my eyes, as my cock strains against the fabric of my trousers and tries to get closer to the person who really owns it.

"That's one," I say, pulling back the slightest bit to breathe in the Charlotte-scented air. Then I start in again, this time slowly teasing her sheath with my finger, playing with her inner folds and pressing gently against the edges of her until she's trying to drop herself onto my finger, until she's making mumbling, fussy noises as she chases my touch with her hips. Finally I indulge her whining and press all the way inside, pulling my mouth away so that I can look up at her as she writhes on my hand.

"You wish it was my cock, don't you?" I say in a low voice. "You wish you were impaled on me, feeling every throb of me. Every inch of me."

"Too many inches," she complains, but the hitch of excitement in her voice betrays how little of a complaint it actually is. "You're abnormal down there."

"Built for you," I say. The honesty and longing in my voice must tug at her, because she blinks down at me with those raincloud eyes. "Every part of my body was built for you."

"You don't believe that," she says, but she sounds a little uncertain. "You don't believe in those kinds of things."

"I do now," I whisper, leaning back in to kiss around my finger as it works inside her. "I do after the last four years without you."

"As if you've been pining. Please." She tries to scoff, but it's at the same time I add a second finger, and so it comes out as a moan instead.

I'm not wounded by this, but only because there's nothing left to wound. I close my eyes and rest my forehead against her stomach. "I can't sleep," I confess, my lips brushing against her intimate skin as I talk, as if I'm confiding into her body. "I can barely work; I can barely even tolerate *thinking* about work because it reminds me of you. I had to stop drinking because I drank too much with you gone. And I hate every person I see that isn't you."

"Except for the people you fuck."

It's a fair comment—before her, fucking was as necessary to me as eating, as digging—and my particular tastes usually entailed transactional liaisons with a myriad of partners. When one wanted to be worshipped in bed, one had to be careful only to find lovers who wanted to worship. Or more plainly put, I only inflicted myself on the willing. Those people whose tastes matched mine. But then I met Charlotte, and Charlotte became my taste, she become the only taste worth having.

"I haven't fucked anyone in four years, Charlotte. Since the day I met you, you've been it for me. Even in your absence, you've been it."

I say this into her skin, breathing the truth into her secret places as I continue to fuck her with my fingers, but she still hears me. She uses her fingers in my hair to pull my head back so she can search my face.

"What about your date at the gala?"

"A colleague."

"She kissed you."

I lift up a shoulder as I stare up at her. "Katie would like there to be more between us, but there's not. I don't push her away in public so I can spare her the embarrassment, but I've made it very clear that's all she can expect from me."

"I don't believe you," she says, but I know she does, I know the truth of it is etched into every part of my face.

"It doesn't matter," I say, looking up at her. "Whether you believe it or not, it's true. I was, am, and will always be your temple. Body and mind."

I don't give her a chance to argue about this; instead, I prove my words true by kissing her and then teasing her with my tongue as I work my fingers inside her. I prove my words by drawing another culmination from her adorable, half-uniform-clad body.

I prove to her that our bodies know things our minds don't.

She arches her back as she comes, her ponytail swishing against the wall as she thrashes through it, and before she's even finished contracting on my fingers, I start up again, sucking on her juicy little bud until I can practically feel it throb on my tongue. Throbbing in time to the urgent ache in my cock, which is beyond hard at this point. Tasting her, smelling her, having her slickness all over my fingers . . . watching that flush crawl up her neck as she comes . . .

I have to close my eyes as her third orgasm peaks, because otherwise I'll orgasm too. I might do it anyway, even with my eyes closed—the slightest contact from my trousers against my swollen tip has me rocking my hips—because it's just too much to be tasting her and fingering her all at once. Too much to hear her low cries and gasps.

"One more," I say. "Give me one more."

She's still clamping down on my fingers from the last one, and she tries to push my head away from her. "No," she moans. "I can't. I can't take it."

"You will," I growl. I draw a finger through her pouty seam, and then use the gathered slickness there to press against the pleated rim behind her pussy. "You'll give me my last orgasm, little one. You're through running from me."

The moment my finger breaches her tight rear entrance, she lets out a ragged sob. "Church," she chokes out. "Church. *Fuuuuck.*"

She's filled in both channels now, stretched around my knuckles as I kiss her everywhere, as I use my tongue on her plump button and on the sensitive petals gloving my fingers.

"Keep saying my name," I order her, chancing a look up to see her staring down at me in flushed, rumpled awe. Awe that shoots through my veins like a drug, a pure dose of heady worship going right to my heart and then back out to every square inch of me, sizzling through my bloodstream until my very skin is on fire with it.

"Church," she breathes. "*Church.*"

Which I can't handle. I can't handle her chanting my name like a prayer, not with that open, unshuttered expression on her face, not with her eyes like silver rain. Not with her body hot and wet and swollen with pleasure.

I make an animal noise against her skin as I use my free hand to tear open my trousers and pull my cock free. I shouldn't come, I don't deserve to come, I don't deserve to feel anything other than grateful that she's letting me do this, but as I said earlier, I'm not sure how moral I actually am. Like everything else in me, my morality begins and ends with Charlotte, and when I feel her tremble like a leaf caught in the wind when she realizes I'm beating off, that's all the absolution I need. She always did like it more if I drained myself during oral sex, and she enjoyed watching me handle my needs so much that I'd reward her with it sometimes. A dirty show just for her peeping little heart.

My hips punch forward into my clumsy, left-handed touch as I use my other hand to wring my last climax out of Charlotte.

"Church," she says again. "Oh fuck, Church, please fuck me. Please please please—"

Her broken words are changing into broken cries, and I relish the sound of them, relish the sound of her begging and craving even after three orgasms. I relish it so much that my starved body releases with a shudder and sends long, hot ropes of cum between her legs, marking the wall, her ankle, part of her pants.

It's the first decent climax I've had in four years, and it wrecks me from head to toe. It ends all thought, all movement, all feeling except the dizzying, floating relief of coming home again.

I didn't even realize I'd stopped eating her until my pulses slowed, and now she's grabbing at my hand to fuck her again, her eyes wide and wild at the sight of my cock and also at my seed everywhere and also at my rough, lewd hand between her legs.

"God, I wish I could fuck you," she says in a pant. "Really fuck you. Hours and hours, riding your giant cock until I can't stop coming—" Her own words send her over, and the fourth orgasm detonates through her. The contractions around my fingers are hard and fast and merciless, and she bends forward at the waist, curling over me as she grips my hair hard and gasps through the sharp, biting pleasure of it.

She cries my name a final time—*Church*—as her body wrings itself free of all the adoration she's soaked up from my touch. Everything is wet and sex-smelling and the pain in my scalp is nothing compared to the jagged joy I feel at seeing and feeling her like this—utterly carnal and completely euphoric. In a state of Church-induced rapture. And then her knees give out, and even though I can catch her before she falls, we end up rolling to the floor in a tangle of legs and arms and expensive wool and cheap uniform polyester.

She blinks down at me with something like bemusement, like she's just awoken from some kind of spell and can't remember how we got here. And I can see it—I can see the very moment self-loathing darkens her eyes and pulls at the nibble-worthy corners of her mouth. She's angry with herself for succumbing to me again. It makes *me* feel angry to witness —angry with myself and her and with everything—and I wish I could just *atone* once and for all, no matter the price. All my money, my property, a finger, a kidney—anything, I would pay any cost, because nothing is as costly as being without her.

Curls the color of white gold have worked their way free from her ponytail and now fly free around her face. They beg to be pulled and I ache to pull them.

I reach up, wind a curl around my finger, and tug.

Her lips part, putting my favorite freckle on delicious display, and then her eyes flutter and widen as the familiar cocktail of pain-induced neuropeptides and hormones lace her blood. Adrenaline, endorphins, dopamine, oxytocin— our altar wine.

I tug again for the sheer pleasure of it, for the drop in my own blood pressure, my own dopamine and oxytocin hits, for the deeper and beyond-chemical joy of seeing her release her clenched grip on her thoughts and hurts and sink completely into the here and now with me. Fuck, I love her. I love her when she wants to murder me, I love her when she resists me, I love her when she surrenders to me. If I were a cleric and not an academic—one of the faithful instead of whatever the skeptical but obsessed fuck I am— this is how I would feel about God too. Full of so much love and adoration that I'd do anything right now to show her, any scourging or fasting she asked.

"You asshole," she whispers, and then fists her hands in my sweater and rolls to the side, so that she's on her back and yanking me over top of her so that I'm braced on my forearms and caging her with muscle and will.

"You missed this," I tell her. I don't need to ask. One

doesn't pull a Dominant ex-lover on top of them if one doesn't miss it.

"You asshole," she repeats, but her eyes are shining with tears. She tries to look away, but there's nowhere to turn her head that isn't into my arms, so it's more a nuzzle than an escape.

Tenderness—the thing I've only ever felt with her— surges up inside me. "You know this is what I meant when I said I wanted to be your temple," I say, fingers finding her hair and stroking the silk there. "The temple to keep you and shelter you and protect you. The temple you could come to for safety and hope and rest. I wanted *this*," and I tighten my arms and legs around her to make my point. That if there was a way I could carry her through the world tucked up inside of myself, I would do it.

"You just want me to worship you again," she sniffs.

That's undeniably true, even if it's not the only thing that's true. "Well. Yes."

"I knew it."

"That doesn't make me a liar, little supplicant. Temples are for the worshippers, not for the worshipped. Is it so hard to believe that I want to give you this more than I want to enjoy you taking it?"

"You left me," she says into my arm, not looking at me. "You were supposed to promise to be my temple forever and you left me."

This is also undeniably true. "I did."

"Why?" she asks brokenly, finally turning her eyes up to me. They are every cloud I've ever seen, every drop of rain, every lonely puddle in the road. "*Why?*"

It's those eyes that finally break me, that gut me. No longer a knife in the heart but through the soul. And I deserve it, because it's as bad as she believes it to be. It might be worse.

"For work," I answer after all these years, and I want to close my eyes right now, a cowardly move but one that's almost irresistibly tempting right now. Because how pathetic it sounds, how stupid and how utterly mundane. She's waited four years to hear that her fiancé and god was more concerned with keeping the right office in the right building than pledging his love to her.

"For work," she repeats, looking confused. "Church, we fucked for a year before the wedding. I wasn't even your student that semester. If you were really worried about work, then why propose? Why go through the whole song and dance of helping me find a venue? Paying for my dress?"

"You would have been my student again," I point out, even though it doesn't matter now. But with our department the way it was and with Charlotte as clever and driven as she was—and with me as possessive as I was—it would have been inevitable. In the classroom or on a dig—she would have been mine again. And I would have made sure it was so, because I never did trust anyone else with the jewel that is my Charlotte's mind. "But that you *had* been, that you were still enrolled at the university, that was damning enough. And I didn't realize it until the director told me."

Her brows pull together. "The director?"

"He came to my flat the morning of the wedding. You may remember that he was dating my sister at the time—and it was my sister who took the liberty of calling my guests and telling them the wedding was off before I knew anything about it."

Her eyes close for a moment. "So that's why none of your guests were there."

"Yes. And he persuaded me that it would be the end of

my career in every meaningful sense if I married a student —not to mention it would have ended your career too, before it had ever started."

The furrow between her brow hasn't gone away, and I kiss it because I can't help myself. "I don't see how my career would have been affected."

"Can you not? How many people would've assumed that you'd fucked your way to prominence instead of earning it on your own merit? We'd know differently, but that hardly matters when the doubt would've pervaded every space you worked in. I couldn't lose my work, Charlotte, but just as much, I refused to lose yours. I couldn't bear the thought of stamping out your future just so I could stamp my name on your legal existence." But my hold on her tightens as I consider that none of it mattered anyway. She still lost her future.

"Then why didn't you answer my calls? Why didn't you *show up* to tell me this? Why didn't you face the aborted ceremony with me? Why didn't you find me that night? Why didn't you find me the next day?"

This. I'm ashamed of this almost more than the decision not to show up to my own wedding. I owed her everything, and I especially owed her the truth. "It took me two or three hours to persuade the director not to make our engagement known, even after I decided not to go the wedding. We've never gotten along, him and me, and he was torn between finally having some kind of political leverage over me or being tainted by association, since he was fucking my sister. By the time I'd convinced him not to poison my career and yours, the wedding was long over—it was why I'd sent the car, you understand. Not to be high-handed or dismissive, although I admit I'm often that, but because I was determined to save the future before I fixed the present, and I wouldn't leave him until I had his word he wouldn't tarnish our names."

She searches my face. "I don't forgive you."

"You shouldn't."

"You did it as much as for yourself as you did it for me."

"I did." I bend my head down so I can smell her neck, her hair, nuzzle my cheek against hers. "I'm sorry, Charlotte. It was selfish and hollow and arrogant of me. I thought if I gave up my chase for God, I'd be giving up myself. But of course, I lost myself the minute I gave you up, and it didn't matter. I damned myself that day, and for nothing."

I can feel her breathing underneath me—the fast, panting swell of her ribcage against mine, the thrum of her pulse against my nose as I run it along the column of her neck.

"And that night, I—" I spare telling her the whole truth, the truth of what I became and what I did to my own house as the horror of what I'd done unfolded inside me. I'm still finding shards of glass four years later. "I wasn't fit to come to you. And when I was more composed, I felt you were owed an explanation beyond a phone call. So I came to your flat to find you the next day."

"I went to the library to use the public computers to look for a job," she says. "I wasn't home."

"I waited for a while, but I was—I'm afraid I still wasn't in the right frame of mind." I'd been like a wounded animal that day, snarling and snapping at everything, and I'd dimly recognized in my hurt and anger that I was likely to shred something between us that couldn't be stitched back together. So like an animal in truth, I'd followed my instincts to the water. I watched night blacken the Thames into a slick of oil, reflecting as much light as it swallowed, and I imagined that cold oil as my shame, coating everything inside of me until it was ready to be lit on fire. Charred to oblivion because everything already felt charred without Charlotte in my arms. Worse than charred.

A world without my little one was a world too dead to burn.

"And I came to find you the next day," she recalls, and I think of a memory colder than that night by the Thames.

"Yes, you did."

At the time, I'd been still too raw, still too arrogant to consider that it was truly the end. She'd walked into my office and set the engagement ring on my desk, and a desperation like I've never known clawed hold of me.

"*You can put that ring anywhere you'd like, but you're still mine.*"

"*I believed that until two days ago, Church. I don't think I believe anything right now, especially since you won't tell me why.*"

Panic. Terror. Shame.

If I told her why, she'd leave. She'd leave and she'd never come back.

Fear boiled in my veins as I tried to convince her and deflect from the terrible truth at the same time.

"We don't need a wedding, Charlotte, nor a marriage nor a mortgage together to prove what we have."

"We don't have anything. Not anymore."

I'd kissed her then, getting to my feet and hauling her into my arms, feeling her shiver and cling to me just as she always did. Feeling her mouth open to mine and accept me. "I acknowledge I've fucked up, little one, but you can't lie to yourself about what we have or don't have. I still need you in my bed and you still need to be there. The rest we can figure out in time."

"I won't go to another church alone," she said against my lips.

The mere mention of what she suffered at my hands made

my bones ache and my body throb. "Maybe churches aren't for us. But my bed is. But this is."

I pulled her back to my mouth and she let me. She let me take a deep, lingering kiss.

Because it was her kiss goodbye.

"I came by for more than giving back the ring," she said, breaking our kiss. "I'm leaving."

I tightened my arms around her. "We'll leave together. Go to my flat. We can work things out there."

"Not leaving your office," she clarified. "Leaving London. Leaving the UK. I'm going back home."

"Home?" I asked, agitated. "Explain yourself, Charlotte, because your home is with me."

She pushed away from me. "There's nothing to explain. I'm going to America and I'm never going to see you again."

I think even then I still hadn't truly believed her, not really. But within a week her flat was empty and she was unenrolled from UCL. She was gone. And the only comfort I had was that somewhere across the ocean, she was fulfilling the promise of that brilliant mind. A promise that was at least undimmed by a connection with me. If nothing else, I spared her that.

"So now you know," I tell her. "I didn't want to tell you, then or last night, because it was so incredibly foolish of me. Selfish, and unforgivably so. But you deserved the truth as much as you deserved my shame, and I didn't give it to you. I'm so sorry, little one. I owed it to you, just as I owe you so much else."

All at once, all the fight seems to leave her. She closes her eyes, her body going still beneath mine. "Now I know," she murmurs, as if to herself. "Now I know."

I drop my forehead to her cheek, and for a moment, we just breathe. Joined together in this wound I gave her.

I know it can't last. We're cold and sticky and tangled, and I haven't forgotten that she needs to get back to work, but the very idea of separating from her *again* has me miserable. I curl my fingers in her cheap work shirt and root through her curls to bury my nose in her scent. She smells clean and floral, like she's just removed a crown of flowers from her hair, and I can't get enough of it.

"I have to go," she says.

"You didn't even murder me. Would you still like to?"

She sighs, and it's not a happy sigh or an amused sigh—or any kind of good sigh. It's the sigh of someone so hurt and so tired that each breath feels like work.

"No, Church," she says wearily. "I don't want to murder you."

I raise up so I can look down at her. A tiny flame of hope curls in my chest. "You don't?"

"That doesn't mean I forgive you," she says pointedly. "And I would like very much never to see you again after this."

I stare down into her perfect face—pert and freckled and stubborn. Can I give her my absence? Now that I know she's here in London? That she's been suffering?

Was I ever capable of it?

Am I a moral man?

Can I be for her?

"Is that what you want from me? Is that the *only* thing you want from me?"

Fuck, this feels worse than bleeding out, than burning, than emptiness and ashes. This is bleeding *in*, this is growing something brand new, just for her. And it hurts. It hurts worse than anything, because before I had no choice, but now I'm agreeing. I'm agreeing to lose her once again.

She hesitates, then the stubbornness reasserts itself in the pull of her mouth and the jut of her chin. "Yes."

"Then you have my word."

She narrows her eyes up at me. "Nothing's ever this easy with you."

Jesus Christ. *Easy?* She thinks this is going to be *easy?* I push up to my feet, wrapping my hands around her elbows and setting her on her own feet in the process. "There's nothing easy about this, Charlotte," I tell her in a sharp voice. "If I had my way, you'd be over my fucking shoulder right now, and I'd be hauling you to my bed where you belong. I'd have you trussed up and so thoroughly fucked that the only thing you would want to do next is nestle into my arms and sleep. I'd be with you when you woke up—then and every day after—and you would go back to the things that made you smile, and you'd stop all this nonsense." I nod at her uniform shirt.

Her face, which had been rapt during my little speech, now grows mulish.

"It's my nonsense, Church. And you're *not* going to have it your way. Even gods have to acknowledge free will," she says, yanking out of my touch.

"Am I still your god then?"

"I don't belong to you anymore, dickhead. There's your answer."

The laugh that leaves my lips is broken and dry. "That may be true, but don't you see it doesn't matter? I belong to you, sweet genius. You've made me your own, and your body feels it even now. Or are those nipples still hard for someone else?"

Spots of color rouge up her cheeks as she starts setting herself to rights. It's hard to say if she's angry with my observation or flushing in response to my heavy cock, which is semi-erect even as I zip my trousers closed. Her eyes follow the movement with unmistakable hunger, but her voice shakes with emotion when she says, "This can't happen again. This *won't* happen again."

I take a long moment to answer, smoothing my clothes and then tucking her curls back behind her ears. She wants to bat me away, I can see, but the minute my fingertips touch her face, her eyes close and her lips part. Drugged like an initiate into esoteric mysteries. Power flowing from me into her, and then back into me again.

"I am your temple no matter what. Your god, your own. When you need me, I'll be there."

A slow shiver moves through her, a dimpling in her chin like she might cry—something I feel like seven thousand arrows—and then she tugs herself away.

"Goodbye, Church."

"Wait."

I have no right to this, I know, and I know more than anything she wants me gone. And I'll go and stay gone, even though I know exactly what ash-dusted tomb I'm consigning myself to—but before I do, I have to know.

"How did this happen, Charlotte?" I ask. "Did you need help finding a job after you graduated?" The thought is actually painful, that she needed help I could have so easily given, and she didn't ask it of me. "Do you still need help? I know you don't want to see me, but I can still—"

She jerks her head to the side, silencing me. "I don't need help," she says tightly. "I'm *fine*."

"You're not." It's shitty and over-familiar of me, maybe. But it's one thing to have work you choose and another thing entirely to have your choices taken away. And everything about her vibrates with the pain of having her choices stripped from her.

She glares again, but she doesn't contradict me.

"I won't apologize for having the audacity to be right, little one."

Her gaze flares to a molten silver and I think for a moment that she's going to shove right past me without answering, that she's going to leave without dignifying my intrusion with a response—but all at once, the anger goes out of her and her shoulders slump. Her eyes drop to the floor and she takes in a long breath that seems to do nothing to make her feel better.

If I thought she looked tired before—hurt, fatigued, alone—then I see it clearly now. The toll her life has taken on her. It's like dying all over again to see it, but of course that's nothing compared to hearing what she says next.

"I didn't need help finding a job after I graduated because I *didn't* graduate. I couldn't—I couldn't even finish the semester. I came back from what was supposed to be our wedding to discover that my father—" she grits out the word with a lifetime of bitterness behind it "—had stolen everything we had and left. Just . . . left. Me and my brother and our flat and everything."

Rage—clean and pure—whitens my vision until I force myself to take a breath. "He abandoned you?"

Simply left his children? One, a college student who was still finding her equilibrium after he'd uprooted the family from America to come back to his own country, and the other, a literal child who had years left of school?

Charlotte cuts a look at me. "Sound familiar? Seems to be a theme with the men in my life."

I wish I could say that shame erases the rage, that I'm humble enough to accept that I can't stand in judgement of others given my own past—but alas. I still want to fling her father into the river.

"I haven't talked to him since then, and I have no idea where he is. I managed to get legal custody of Jax and tried to keep things normal for him, but . . ." She looks down again. "I couldn't afford to stay in school and pay for the rent and food and everything else. I have to work two jobs as it is, just to scrape by, and to have to manage tuition on top of that? And even without tuition, whatever's left of my time belongs to Jax. Helping him with school, making sure he's ready for his exams, taking him to art studio and his flute lessons and keeping an eye on his group of friends . . ."

She puffs out a breath. "Maybe my father thought because I was marrying someone, we didn't need him around anymore. Or maybe I'm giving him too much credit by imagining he thought about us at all. But the upshot is that I was completely and utterly alone. I had nothing, and I had no one, and yeah, it fucking sucks that I couldn't finish school and follow the path I wanted. But you know what? I'm fucking *here*. My brother is here. We're sheltered and fed and safe, and that's because of me. That's because of what I gave up and what I worked for, and I refuse to let you make me feel like shit about it, okay? I'm better than that. My efforts are better than that."

She is. They are.

And I am nothing. Nothing in the shape of a man.

"Goodbye, Church," she says again, and this time I don't stop her.

This time I let her go.

5

Charley

Undefended and alone, now the girl must make a nest of pillows and blankets to protect herself. Tomorrow, the harsh London wilderness will be waiting. But tonight the girl must retreat and recoup. And cry.

I know things have to be bad if I'm Attenboroughing myself. Dazed and dizzy from three solid hours of sobbing, I manage to fake my way through dinner and homework with Jax, and then I collapse into a fitful sleep. Tomorrow is a double shift at Tesco, and the day after will be Tesco plus a catering gig, and I don't *have time* for Church to be in my thoughts like this. For his words to be swimming through my veins and crawling inside of my heart.

Since the day I met you, you've been it for me.

Do I believe that? Does it matter even if I do?

I am your temple no matter what.

When you need me, I'll be there.

Liar. He's a liar. He wasn't there when I needed him, he wasn't there when he said he would be.

Except you never gave him a chance to be after the day of the wedding, a voice reminds me. *You made sure he thought you were gone—you made sure he couldn't be there for you at all.*

Well, I refuse to feel bad about that. He did the worst thing, and when someone does the worst thing, they don't get second chances. Especially when that worst thing was to save their career.

And yours, the voice says. Which makes me scowl. My career was lost anyway, and besides, I'm not interested in forgiving him for choosing *anything* over me. Not when there were seventeen thousand other ways he could have handled things. Number one of which was to have told the director to fuck off and then shown up to our goddamn wedding.

But you know what it means to him. His job is the literal manifestation of his desire to find God. Can you really blame him for that?

I want to. And I think I do, but in order to keep the blame bigger than the sympathy, I have to forget what an amazing teacher he was. How carefully he mentored all of his students and the pains he took to help each one of them improve. I have to forget about how he lit up on a dig site, becoming smiley and boyish and excited; I have to forget the awe in his voice and the humility in his face when he cupped fragments of forgotten worlds in his hands.

But I will forget it. I will if it's the last thing I ever do. I'm not going to forgive him, and I'm not going to keep thinking about his cruel mouth and glittering eyes and smoky voice. I'm *definitely* not going to remember the jolt of pure rightness I felt when he told me that he belonged to me, that he wanted to be my temple again. I won't remember the gouging agony in his expression as I told him exactly how hard the last four years have been, and I won't remember his stern words when he refused to let me hide my pain from him.

I won't apologize for having the audacity to be right, little one.

Nope. Not interested. Still a mean little bunny. Still smarter than falling in love with a broken, miserable god. I will forget the last two nights ever happened and go back to the safer—if lifeless—way things were before, and that's just how it's going to be.

***

EXCEPT THE NEXT MORNING, I wake up with a tender pussy and my heart in my throat. I wake up with Church's words still whispering in my mind.

Am I cursed? Is this what a curse is?

It feels very Greek to me, very much like I'm the victim of some capricious divine whim. Doomed to long for someone who fucked me over.

Hungry for the touch of someone who thinks me worthless.

Okay, maybe that's not . . . *entirely* fair.

Church was never the kind of man to be interested in something inferior; he didn't waste his time with anything cheap or dull. He thought me brilliant and adept and *his*. And I know all that because he told me so. And the only time Church ever lied was the day he failed to show up for our wedding, and even then, he didn't lie with his words, only his actions. In fact, for all his cruelty, all his arrogance, and all his ice, Church was always unfailingly, painfully honest.

Maybe he's being honest now?

I'm so sorry, little one.

I am your temple no matter what.

It doesn't matter, I tell myself. It doesn't matter how sorry he is, it doesn't matter how right and alive I felt with him yesterday, it doesn't matter how he sees me exactly as I need to be seen.

Because I'll never forgive him for not seeing me when it mattered.

I get dressed with a huffy forcefulness, as if that will prove to some invisible audience that I'm really done thinking about Church and not at all noticing how my well-pleasured body twinges with every movement. I see my brother off to school, and then I stop by the landlord's flat on the ground floor to drop off this month's rent before I go in to work.

Roksana, my landlord, narrows her eyes when she opens the door to me. "You can't take it back," she says with a sniff. "I've already started spending it. Repairs, if you must know."

"Uh," I say, glancing behind me to make sure there isn't some other tenant she's talking to. Seeing no one, I decide to pretend the last ten seconds didn't just happen. "I brought this month's rent for you. I'm sorry I didn't get it to you on Friday, but I got home from work so late, and I didn't want to wake you—"

She doesn't take the envelope from me. Instead she sniffs again. "You can't take it back."

"Take what back?"

"If you want to add it to what you've already paid this morning, you can, but you can't take it back and then pay me for only this month instead. Like I told you, I've already spent a lot of it."

"Roksana, I think there must be some kind of mistake. I haven't paid you yet."

She narrows her eyes even more and sucks her teeth. "First thing this morning, I was on the phone with a man who seemed to know you. I assumed it was a boyfriend at first, but he was quite cold with me, I'll have you know, and very impatient. I thought then maybe he was a solicitor of yours, or a banker. He wired the next twelve months' rent right into my account."

Quite cold. Very impatient.

And could drop a year's rent into someone's account at the drop of a hat.

A white, angry static crackles in my vision and my hearing and I can feel it singe the inside of my veins. "He didn't happen to give his name, did he?"

Roksana shrugs. "Church something. Churchwell? Churchhill?"

James Church Cason. My hand fists around the envelope and Roksana glances down at it, shrewd assessment in her gaze. "You could give me that for safekeeping," she says. "In case this Church man changes his mind."

"I think I better hang on to it," I manage, anger coursing through me so hot and bright that I can't even remember why I didn't murder him the last two times I saw him. "If you'll excuse me, I need to make a phone call."

***

THE WALK to work is windy, with that kind of autumnal spatter that can't decide if it wants to rain or what, and it matches my shitty mood perfectly when Church answers my call. A shitty mood that's exacerbated by the fact that I still have his phone number memorized after four years. *What is wrong with me?!*

"What the hell do you think you're doing?" I demand, before he can say a single word. "This is way out of line, even for you."

"Hello, Charlotte," Church says softly.

"Don't *hello, Charlotte* me. You had no right to pay for my rent. *None.*"

"It's a gift," he says. His voice is still soft, but threaded through the words is an unmistakable edge. The one that kept me coming back to Church's bed over and over again—the cold imperiousness that thaws only for me. "It's freely given. I don't expect anything in return, little one." Even with the strange combination of softness and arrogance, honesty still rings through his words. He's telling the truth—or thinks he is.

I still say, "Oh, really?" because that's just who I am.

"Yes, really. I wanted to ease something for you that was in my power to ease, Charlotte. I wanted to make something—anything—better for you and Jax."

I flush with more than anger, although I'm not sure what for. Embarrassment that he so easily peeled back the lid on my shitty, cash-strapped life? Or something much, much more dangerous?

Am I . . . *touched*? That he notices me and thinks of me? Am I turned on by the fact that he still wants to care for me? Am I grateful that he picked the single biggest source of my misery to ameliorate?

Ugh.

Maybe.

Stupid bunny.

My footsteps become more like stomps as my irritation

with myself spills over to him again. "You still should have asked, you interfering prick."

The silence following my insult scratches at me, if I'm honest. I've always been colorful with my language around him—prick, bastard, asshole, *arse*hole if I was in the mood to make fun of him—and I've never stepped back from provoking him. But my little rebellions and challenges were always met with scrumptious wrath; more often than not, I was hauled over his lap and spanked until I was begging to be fucked. Sometimes he would wait to punish me for my brattiness, letting the anticipation worm its way under my skin until I was near crazed with it, and then finally tying me to his bed and tracing rebuke all over my body with his tongue and teeth.

And yes, okay, sometimes I provoked him *because* I wanted some spanking and bondage. Sometimes a girl needs to savor the sweet displeasure of her god, what can I say?

But right now, he's saying nothing. He's not purring sexy threats into my ear, he's not dryly musing aloud about whether his bratty supplicant needs to be bitten or ridden or both. He's quiet and I find that I hate it.

"Aren't you going to say something?" I demand.

Church sighs. "What is there to say? That the only thing that kept me on this side of sane for the last four years was the mistaken hope that you were in the States building a life for yourself? That knowing you've been suffering, that you've been alone, that every day has not only been a struggle but a slow starvation of the things that used to feed you—that the knowledge is fucking damning? And I can barely swim through the hours knowing it?"

The pain in his voice saws right through me, and I stop walking.

"I don't care if I'm the villain. I don't mind being the bastard. If I can do anything to ease your suffering, if you sleep better for just one hour of just one night, then it is worth you hating me more than you did before."

The insides of my eyelids burn a little at that, and I duck my head so no passersby will notice how fiercely my chin is wobbling. The words *I don't think I hate you* are on the tip of my tongue and they sting more than the unshed tears.

"You can't atone for what you did," I say in a whisper instead.

"I'm not trying to, Charlotte, not anymore. I know I can't buy your forgiveness. Now all that's left for me is to live with myself and what I've done."

It's his raw but honest admission that pushes the first sob out of me.

"Little one," he says, sounding as broken as I feel. "Are you crying? Are you that furious with me?"

"Yes. No." Another wet, gasping sob. "I don't know, Church. I don't know. Some moments I think I hate you, and then other moments, like right now, I wish you were here."

"That's the pain talking," he says gently. "You don't really."

The tears are flowing fast and freely now, mingling with the cool drops of rain. "You have no right to say what part of me is talking and what isn't," I say, knowing it sounds like nonsense and not caring.

"Of course," he murmurs.

"And you have no right to decide what will ease any of my sufferings," I mumble.

He hums in agreement, a soothing noise that immediately makes me feel safe and small and loved.

I'm reminded of all the times I showed up in his office, shaky and exhausted from a night guarding Jax from my father's drunkenness, a sleepless night sitting against the inside of our bedroom door, terrified that my dad would beat it down at any moment. Me, I looked too much like his dead wife to scream at, but Jax? Jax was the perfect target. And Jax only had me to protect him. Which meant once or twice a month, I'd see Jax safely to school and then stagger to the one place *I* felt safe.

With Church.

He'd take one look at me and then somehow I'd end up in his lap, cradled against his chest as I cried myself to sleep right there in his office, and then I'd wake up on the settee he kept for students to sit on during meetings.

After the second time it happened, he took out one of the bookshelves in his office and bought a long sofa to replace the settee, so that then I'd wake up several hours later on plush cushions with a pillow under my head and a soft blanket pulled over me. Groggy but protected. Cared for. And he listened when I begged him not to get involved, although he did inform me that the next time my father did anything more than look at my brother, he'd be stepping in.

For a kinky, autocratic monster, he was always careful with the boundaries I needed him to be careful with. He only invaded the parts of my heart marked for invasion.

I miss him. I don't hate him and I can't forgive him and I miss him.

"Church?"

"Yes, Charlotte?"

"Will I still be your little supplicant even now? Now that I've told you to stay away? And now that you can't ever make up for what you did?"

His voice is pure Church when he answers—like the still, small voice Elijah heard outside the cave: quiet and boundless all at once. "Always. You have the right to ask me to stay away, but there is one thing you can never ask of me, and that is for me to stop loving you. It would be easier to ask me to stop breathing."

I feel like I can't breathe myself. I certainly can't speak. I can't even cry properly; the tears are just leaking out now without any effort from me.

He makes another one of those noises that makes me feel like I'm tucked against him, listening to the steady, reassuring beat of his heart while he sifts through my hair. "I love you too much not to give you what you need. I won't approach you, I won't call, and you are certainly entitled to give back the money if you need."

The rain comes down harder now, hard enough that it makes it difficult to hear his final words. But I do hear them. I hear them and begin weeping in earnest.

"Be well, little one," he says, love and arrogance winding through his words in that way I adore so much. "You, Charlotte Tenpenny, smartest and bravest person I know, will always be my heart and my faith."

And then he hangs up.

6

Charley

I make it a week.

Barely.

The morning of the seventh day, I'm caught in a slurry of UCL students, tourists, and commuters pushing impatiently out of Euston Station as I make my way to the archaeology building to find Church. Gordon Square is spitting wet leaves in shades of red and gold onto the street, and I try not to think about how many peaceful hours I spent in that damp and rustling stretch of trees and grass while I was a student here. I try not to remember what it was like to stare at the window I knew belonged to Church's office, a smile on my lips to match the secret tucked away in my chest.

I mumble apologies as I push past the students and make my way into the building, ducking through hallways filled with chatter about soil micromorphology and ceramic petrography. I pass by labs and lecture rooms; I catch the familiar scents of coffee and climate-controlled air. Longing for this place fills me up like heavy water as I climb the stairs.

I was happy here.

I could have been happier still.

No sense in rehashing all that now. I'll be back. If not here, then somewhere else, and I'll kick ass there instead. I'll make up for all the lost time and then some.

Bolstered by the thought, I reach Church's floor, taking deep breaths in an effort to steady my thumping heart. What will he say when he sees me? Will he be angry? Will he be frustrated? After all, it was me who demanded space, and now here I am waltzing right into his.

He's a smart man, I remind myself. He'll understand that just for today, I need to reopen communication, and anyway, if *he'd* asked for space, then of course I would respect that. But he didn't, and a not-so-small part of me flutters at the thought that he didn't ask for it because he wants me to change my mind. Because he wants to be open and available in case I do.

Which I am.

Because I have to give the rent back.

I wish it was because of pride. I wish I could say it's because I've taken care of Jax and myself *just fine* for four years, and I don't need to ruin my streak with some man's guilt-money. I wish I could say that making any part of my life easier on his account irrevocably taints my honor and it just can't be borne.

But none of that's true. I've been poor my whole life and desperately so for the last four years; if everything else about me and Church were different, I'd take his money just like I took all those orgasms from him a week ago and walk away without looking back.

No, it's a bigger sin than pride that compels me today.

I can admit it now, after this last awful week. I love him. Stupid bunny that I am, I love him and crave him and want to forgive him. And maybe . . . maybe I already have forgiven him? There's a difference between forgiveness and trust, right?

I can forgive him without trusting him, I can let go of my pain without giving him the power to hurt me again.

The problem is that I want more than just to forgive, bloodlessly and from a distance.

I want to curl up in his lap and sob into his strong chest. I want to be angry with him, I want to hate him, and I want him to be strong enough to take it, to hold me while I cry over the hurts he gave me.

And then I want every dirty, sacred moment I missed with him over the last four years. Every moment I'm owed.

But how can I want that without betraying the girl he hurt? I demand of myself. *How can I want to be his again without betraying myself?*

I can't.

But I also can't have his gift haunting me. It's like the ghost of his smoky, spicy scent; it's like the still-warm imprint of him in my bed. So long as the money is there, Church is there. And every moment free from worry is now laden with memories of him—the midnight eyes, the harsh mouth. The *words.*

I am your temple no matter what.

There is one thing you can never ask of me, and that is for me to stop loving you.

Fuck, I have to give that money back. I have to be free of this.

Church's office is tucked away on an upper floor, on the side overlooking Gordon Square, and it's impossible not to have a Pavlovian response as I approach it, even after all this time. My heart thuds wildly, my belly feels hot and tight, everywhere my skin begs for touch, for teeth. Sometimes I'd be summoned here, sometimes I'd surprise him, but more often than not, I was hauled here by the elbow and then covered with his trembling body the minute the door clicked shut.

That infinite god-hunger of his. How I delighted in being his sacrifice over and over and over again . . .

Fitting that it ended at a literal altar.

Maybe it doesn't have to end, a traitorous hope murmurs. *Maybe he'll spread you out on his desk and . . .*

I ache with the thought—a deep, shuddering ache that only Church can soothe. I should leave. I shouldn't knock on his door like this, wet and ready for him to ease his heavy cock inside me, but I am knocking, I am opening the door, knowing full well if he so much as looks at me, I'll fall to his feet and beg for just one more minute of supplication. One more act of worship.

But when I open the door, it doesn't reveal my flawed deity, but an utterly empty room. There're no books on the shelves, there's no antique desk with a drawer for the little depravities we couldn't help but indulge on campus. There's no sofa for a scared, exhausted girl to crash on after keeping watch over her brother, and there's no basket next to it for a soft blanket to cover her with.

There's nothing and no one.

Church is gone.

But when? How? *Why*?

This should be the one constant—the one thing that holds the universe together.

Church teaches. Church teaches so Church can chase God through muddy fields and underneath crumbling tells. This is his life, his only passion. His calling.

And he's fucking brilliant at it.

"Looking for someone?" a voice asks from behind me.

I'm frozen in the doorway, almost unwilling to turn around and leave this moment of shock behind because I know what comes after it will be worse. But I do turn around, and when I do, I see the director. Officious and reedy and pinch-lipped.

It's the same director who told Church he couldn't go through with our wedding.

I have no idea if he recognizes me or not, and in this moment, I couldn't give a rat's ass. "Where is he?" I demand. "Where are his things?"

"He left," the director says. His words hold just the faintest whiff of smugness, but there is a tightness to his face that suggests he's unhappy too. Which makes sense. Whatever his personal feelings towards Church, he just lost the brightest star in his institute, not to mention the best teacher. Church's students went on to do great things—good-for-alumni-brochure things—and most importantly, people left his classes changed for the better. Smarter and more perceptive and more imaginative than they were before.

He's an amazing teacher.

And he's not here.

"He *left*?" I repeat, as if the director must be mistaken. "He wouldn't leave. This is—this is everything to him. It's everything he ever wanted."

The director shrugs gracelessly. "Apparently not."

"But . . ." I turn and look back into the office. Outside the windows, Gordon Square is wet and bright with autumn colors. Behind me are the faint noises of doors closing, people murmuring, someone rolling a cart down the hall. This was his world. His entire world was this place.

"He left," the director repeats, "in the middle of term and with no notice. I told him he'd never find a position again quitting like this, but he said he didn't care." The director scoffs. "Probably with as much money as he's got, he doesn't have to care."

I'd really like to tell this guy to eat a bag of dicks, because this job was the *only* thing Church cared about— even more than he cared about me. He was frequently impatient with the bureaucracy, with the labyrinthine politics, with how difficult it was to secure permission and funding to do the things he *really* loved, but never, ever in the time we were together did he raise the possibility of quitting. *Never.* So what could have changed?

Me?

No. Surely not. Church isn't stupid; I told him he couldn't atone. And he's not a liar—he told me he wasn't trying to.

So then why would he do this idiotic, self-destructive, selfish, cowardly thing? How could he do this to the students who needed him? How could he do this to *himself*? How could he rob himself of his future and his passion and the only part of him that resembled a soul?

I turn back to the director, and whatever is in my face has him taking a step back.

"Listen, madam," he says, "there's no need to be angry with *me*, it was entirely his decision—"

"Where is he now?" I snap, not interested in playing nice.

"I presume at home? He cleaned out the office yesterday—"

I'm already pushing past him to get to the stairs, and within a few minutes, I'm hopping down the stairs to Russell Square Station and catching a Piccadilly line train. I'm not sure what my plan is—I'm not sure I really had a plan in the first place, even before I knew he'd quit teaching—but I'm certain some yelling is going to be involved. Maybe some light murder is back on the table.

I mean, really. What the hell? After leaving me at the literal altar for this job, he's not going to keep it? After making me the burnt offering for his career, he's just going to walk away?

Screw. That.

He is going to get that job back and he is going to fulfill his promise as a professor and as an archaeologist. It makes no sense for him to waste his mind and his gifts like this. It makes about as much sense as me dropping out of school, except in my case, I literally had no other choice. Yet he's awash in choices, he's buried up to his neck in them.

So why *this* choice?

Yes, murder is back on the table now. And this time it's not for hurting me, it's for hurting himself.

When I get to his Belgravia townhouse—a graceful rise of white Georgian architecture set against the frowning sky —the door is hanging open as a young man lugs photography equipment inside. A crisp-looking woman in perfectly hemmed wide-leg trousers is talking to someone else on the front steps.

"We should wait for a sunny day for the rooftop photos," the person says back to her. They seem to be looking through the weather app on their phone, oblivious to the woman's eye roll.

"In October?" she asks impatiently. "I think we'll be waiting a while. And he wants the listing up tomorrow. We're doing it today."

The person on their phone sighs but accepts her decision. "I suppose if he's listing it under market value anyway . . ."

The woman nods, like this is all something the person should have already put together.

Jesus Christ. He's selling his house.

The woman—his estate agent, I presume—finally catches me hovering on the sidewalk, assessing in an instant that I am not a potential buyer for a multimillion-pound home and narrowing her eyes at me. "Can I help you?"

I'm too shocked and angry to put on the dimple-and-freckles act for her. "Yes. I'm looking for James Cason."

If the agent is surprised a girl in a sweater dress and scuffed boots knows the owner of the house, she doesn't show it. "He's not here. We're preparing the house for market, as you can see, and he told us he'd spend the day at his second home to give us space to work. And no—" she adds, seeing me open my mouth "—I don't know when he'll be back. Perhaps you could try calling him."

"Perhaps I could," I say, already walking away. I don't need to call him, because I already know where he is. He doesn't have a second home in the city, but he does have one place here that he loves above all others.

"Thank you," I tell the agent over my shoulder, and then I retrace my steps all the way back to the Tube and back to Russell Square Station.

7

Church

There was a practice among the ancient Celts.

They would make swords inlaid with gold and precious stones. They would polish stone axe heads for thousands of hours until the stones gleamed like glass. They would make intricate necklaces and bracelets and rings. Anything could work really, so long as it was very difficult to make and too precious to lose.

And then they would break these things.

Swords were curled into circles, axes cracked in half. Jewelry was bent and scored and cut. The objects weren't just marred, they weren't just broken—they were *ruined*. They were killed until there was no question of them ever being useful again.

Then these beautiful, dead gifts were given to the waters, to the lakes and rivers and bogs where the gods lived. An offering. A sacrifice.

Sometimes, if I close my eyes and I still my breathing, I can imagine the flashing and glinting of the bent swords as they drop through the water to the depths below. I can see the last glimmer of the necklaces as they slip into the shadows.

The final gasp of things that were made only to be broken, things made only to be given up to dark and never seen again.

I wonder if this is Charlotte and me—except if it is, then who is the slayer and who is the offering?

Who did the making and who did the breaking?

***

THE MUSEUM IS QUIET TODAY, which suits me just fine. I drift through the European rooms and then the British rooms, looking at all the torcs and shields that long-dead priests gave to the waters, and I miss Charlotte. I stare at the Sutton Hoo exhibit and glance at the various belts and knives and cauldrons liberated from hoards and burials, and I miss Charlotte. I sit down on a bench and stare at my pointless hands, my empty hands—hands that should be cradling and petting and spanking—and I miss Charlotte.

We're both the offerings, I think tiredly. I broke her, then she broke me.

No. She'd already broken me. From that very first day. From that very first moment right here in the museum. I saw her and then I was bent for her. Cracked and killed. All for Charlotte Tenpenny.

Everything else was just flashes and glimmers in the dark.

I'm not sure how much of the morning I pass in this fashion, haunting the exhibits and missing Charlotte as only a broken thing can, but when I wander over to the Mesopotamia room, I find it empty. The neighboring room is closed for a new case installation, and the exhibit two rooms down is roped off for something that involves a camera crew, and the cumulative effect is that it seems to deter traffic away from Mesopotamia.

I don't mind. I rather like being alone with my agony. It feels fitting.

I'm staring at the relief of Ishtar that started it all when I hear the footsteps. The quick, angry slap of boots on the wood flooring, and before I have a chance to look up, she's excoriating me with her words.

"Just what the *fuck* do you think you're doing?" she hisses, stomping towards me. Her hair is down, making a halo of soft, curling gold around her face, and all her stomping has sent an appealing pink blooming under her freckles. And that lip—God, that lip. Even now, even broken, my body responds to that sinfully freckled mouth like she's already promised it back to me.

She's still striding towards me and berating me all the while, and all I can think about is how beautiful she is. How perfect. The hem of her sweater dress doesn't quite reach the over-the-knee socks she's wearing under her boots, and slivers of pale, freckled thighs tease me with every step. Her dress hugs her body, as if in worship, clinging to her breasts and hips, hanging down to cover her hands to keep them warm. I wish very suddenly that I could keep her hands warm, but I know if I reach out to wrap them in my own, she'll leave, and I don't want her to leave.

I want her to stay here in this dim museum twilight and keep abusing me in that sweet, angry voice of hers. If she wanted to scream at me forever, I would let her happily. With all the relief I could ever feel.

I'm still staring at her with a smile on my face when she reaches me and takes a big breath. She narrows her eyes. "Are you even listening to me?"

I shake my head, daring to reach out and tuck a wild curl behind her ear. "But keep talking, please. I deserve all of it."

She huffs, very adorably, and crosses her arms over her chest. "Your reverse psychology won't work on me."

I just want to gather her in my arms and prop her on my lap and murmur every beautiful thing about her into her ear. I want to spend days memorizing the freckles on her shoulder. I want to spend the rest of my life with my nose buried in the curve of her neck. "Please," I say. My voice is soft, but earnest enough that it makes her hesitate. "Keep going. I want to hear you."

She glares at me a little like she still thinks it's some kind of trick, but then she relents, too furious with me to bottle it inside any longer. "Fine, *professor*," she seethes, sticking a finger against my chest. Warmth blooms from where she's touching me to everywhere else in my body, sending something hotter than heat all the way to the whorls of my fingers and the soles of my feet. Happiness, I think. Joy.

Love.

I want to press my body to hers, my broken heart to her broken heart and just let the jagged edges stab and shred us all over again.

She's still going. "You're going to hear me, because what kind of self-destructive moron leaves the only job they've ever wanted, and I know you're not a liar, and I know you said you weren't trying to atone, so then what could possibly have motivated such a fucked-up decision—and how could you do that to your students and to *yourself*, you're going to be so miserable, and do you want to be miserable? Because I don't see any other way—"

I surrender to the need to touch her, and I take the hand currently against my chest and cradle it in my own. I bring it to my lips and simply touch them there. Her skin against mine. It's heaven.

Her rant is brought to halt by this, and I can feel her pulse speed in her wrist at my touch. I can hear the hitch in her breath as I kiss her knuckle and then her palm and then her fingertip.

"You look like shit," she grumbles, unable to keep scolding me but also unable to completely let it go.

"I know." I say the words against her skin. "I know."

"Church," she whispers. "Why?"

That's been this whole week between us—the *whys*—although I know for her it's been much longer. Four years of *why*, and I'll never be able to make that up to her. I need her to know that as much as I need to savor these last few seconds between us. She'll leave and I'll let her, and then I'll let myself sink into the dark. Find some cottage somewhere and live out the rest of my days as the shattered man I am.

"It wasn't to prove something to you," I tell her, looking up to her face. Her eyes shine with angry tears, and my heart rips a little. "I swear, Charlotte, I swear on everything I've ever cared about. This wasn't a grand gesture. I wasn't trying to—"

I can't finish the words. Because while I'm not trying to win her back, while I know I can never make up for what I've done, my instinct is still to pin her by the wrists to the nearest wall and kiss her breathless. My instinct is still to take her home, cage her with my body, and tell her *mine, mine, mine* until we both believe it again.

So it's very hard to say *I wasn't trying to get you back*, not because it's not true—it is—but because I'll always want her back. Always, until I die, and then even in the realms past death. She is my own soul.

"I wasn't trying to earn your forgiveness or your pity," I say instead, straightening up. I don't let go of her hand, however, and she doesn't make me. "I need you to know that."

"I do know that, *asshole*," she fumes, tears spilling over. "I know that, and that makes it worse, because it means your only other motive was hurting yourself, and I hate it. I hate that you've cut yourself off from the thing you've dedicated your life to."

My thumb can't stop rubbing at the skin of her wrist. If I could stop time, I'd stop it right here—my thumb brushing against her very pulse, her face teary and gorgeous and lit by the carefully muted bulbs of the exhibit cases.

"Why are you looking at me like that?" she sniffles, trying to duck her face away from me. It's habit—and probably a bad one—when I don't let her. I catch her face with my other hand and make it so our eyes meet.

"Looking at you like how?" I murmur. Even though I already know.

"You know how," she mumbles, because she knows that I know. It's why I knew she'd survive me when I first saw her —because she's always seen straight through my games. And then chosen to play along anyway. "All puppy-dog-eyed. And . . ."

She reaches up and touches the edge of my mouth. I think I might expire in agony. I love her so fucking much.

"You're smiling," she says on an exhale, her voice and fingertips trembling. "This is a *smile*."

"I have been known to smile, little one. Especially around you."

She shakes her head, her eyes tracing the curve of my

lips. "No. Not this kind of smile. Not like you're happy when you have every reason *not* to be happy."

I can feel my lips tilt even more against her touch, and I want to nip at her fingers so badly, I want to take one into my mouth and flick my tongue against the tiny whorls and ridges of the tip until she's whimpering for me to tongue her clit. I know any moment this will stop and she will walk away and I will never see her again, but maybe she wouldn't mind one last little bite. One final kiss to last me the rest of my pointless, lonely life.

"You—I told you to stay away from me," she goes on. "I told you I wouldn't forgive you. And then you left your work, which is the only thing you've ever loved. You shouldn't be smiling."

"I'm smiling because I'm looking at you, darling girl."

"But—"

It's my turn to shake my head. "There're no buts, Charlotte. No qualifiers. You are the very expression of the sacred. You are my holiness. Seeing you is like being transfigured, heartbeat by heartbeat, breath by breath, into light itself." A tear slides down her cheek at my words, and I frown at it. "I know there's no act I can lay at your feet to redeem my selfishness, and I almost don't want there to be, because I don't deserve even the comfort that it could be possible. But how could I keep living with the wages of my sins after knowing how much they'd cost you? These last four years, I've been sustaining myself on the lie that you were better off without me. But you weren't. And I can't serve any longer the idol I chose over you. You say my work is the only thing I ever loved, but it was *you*, Charlotte. How could I still pretend to chase God when I'd already let the divine slip through my fingers?"

Another big tear slips down her cheek, and I'm going to

hell, but it'll be worth it for this one stolen taste. I lean in and kiss that tear away, letting the salt bloom on my tongue, and she shivers against me.

"Don't cry," I murmur. "It'll be okay."

I start to pull back, and then she grabs the front of my sweater and twists her fingers in, holding me close. She's still trembling. "It won't be okay," she whispers. "It can't be okay now. Not when I need—"

She stops herself abruptly, and worry twists my guts. She needs something? Is there more financial worry? Is her father back and causing trouble? "Tell me and I'll make it happen. Do you need money? Help? For me to leave right now?"

Her eyes meet mine in a scorch of silver. "I need *you*," she chokes out, and it stuns us both. It stuns me so much that I'm totally unprepared for her to yank me down to her mouth and kiss me like it's the only thing that can keep her alive.

8

Charley

For a few gentle but breathless moments, Church's mouth is pliant against mine. In fact, all of him is pliant—soft and surprised and yielding. I pull him closer to me, and he lets me, and I part his lips with my own to taste him, and he lets me. I slide my hands up so that I can wrap my arms around his neck and I kiss all of my need into him, all of my anger and hurt and loneliness and longing. The horrible tangle of *wanting* to hate him, but knowing I'll always, always love him.

And he lets me, he lets me, he lets me.

If I hadn't seen the truth in his shattered gaze, if I hadn't heard the honesty in his tired, smoky voice, then I would feel it in his body now: he didn't expect this. He didn't expect anything from me.

He meant everything he said.

His hands are slow and shaking as they touch my back, his body is totally frozen against mine. Through our clothes, I feel the pound of his heart, and when I break our kiss and open my eyes, I find his already open, watching me with something beyond awe, something purer than awe, because it's stripped of all hope. It's pure humility, pure adoration.

It's worship.

I used to be the cleverest girl in class, but I'm all out of answers right now. Because he's looking at me like that, his eyes are a deep ocean blue like that, and he's still *smiling* like that.

And what possible answer can I have? To him? To the strange and terrible and undeniable fact that I forgive him? Everyone I know would tell me it's stupid, everyone I know would tell me that he doesn't deserve it, that I deserve better, and logically, it all adds up: he hurt me, therefore fuck him.

But maybe . . . maybe logic isn't all of love. Maybe it isn't even half, maybe not even a quarter. Because I do love him, damn my eyes, and what I wouldn't give for some new kind of logic, a logic that could account for *fuck him* and also *let's fuck him*. A formula that could compute *I love him* and *I can't trust him* and *I don't know how to trust him again* but also *I'd like to try*.

There's no logic like that, there are no answers. Which means I'm only going to listen to the questions right now. Namely, one question.

What is the one thing I know I want with all my heart in this very moment?

That . . . that I do know the answer to, and I pull him back to me for a second kiss.

It's like a match is struck.

Church's pliancy burns clean away and blazes into something else. Something firm and fierce and possessive. *He's* the one to chase my mouth now, he's the one fisting and yanking at my sweater, and he's the one kissing with his whole body: his hands shoving at the hem of my dress, a hard thigh pushing between mine, an arm now banding behind my back so that I can feel his hardness everywhere. His erection, his stomach, his chest. Everywhere he is granite—if granite can be ferocious and greedy and hot.

"Little supplicant," he breathes against my mouth. In just those two words, I hear *him*, my Church, my angry god. And I also hear this new Church, this man so broken with love for me that he won't even pray for atonement because he knows he doesn't deserve it. I hear both versions of him, and I think I love both. I love him both godlike and mortal, I love him in his cold, marble perfection and I love him shattered.

"Please," I kiss-mumble, trying to climb him, wishing I could climb *inside* him, wishing there was something closer than close. And I don't even know what I'm saying *please* to, just that I need to say it, and I need him to hear it. I need him to know that I meant *I need you* in every possible way.

I'm not a small woman, but Church takes me easily in his arms, biting at my jaw and neck as he carries me to the corner of the room. Each bite sends sparks shivering across my skin; each bite reminds me of what I've always needed, which is this. Which is him.

I scan the room as he bites my throat and his hands flex under my thighs. He sets me down and pins me against the side of an exhibit case with his chest and hips, while his hands keep roaming up and down the bare skin of my thighs under my dress.

I twist my head to check that the exhibit room is still empty—we're partially hidden from view, but it wouldn't take someone very long to figure out there's a girl getting felt up in the corner. My turning deprives him of my throat and he growls my name.

"Just making sure no one sees," I say—my words choked

off by a large hand palming my breast and the resulting surge of heat between my legs. As if he knows—he always knows—Church presses his hips in and uses the giant rod of his erection to rub against me.

"Don't I always make sure you're safe?" he asks, fucking me slowly through our clothes. He pushes up my dress so that it's only his trousers and my knickers between us and I groan. "Have I ever let a stranger see what's mine?"

"N-no." My teeth are chattering, and I can't stop shaking. Each grind of his cock against me has my eyes fluttering. "You never let anyone see."

It's the truth. Church had always been as careful as he was insatiable, and as many times as I'd been fucked, fingered, or eaten in public, I'd never been seen. I was never sure if it was because he was possessive or thoughtful or some heady mix of both, but the result was the same: Church took care of me as he took what he wanted from me, and every needy, breathless fuck that we stole in public was as safe as it was urgent.

He rakes his teeth over my throat as I realize he's angled our bodies so that even the security cameras can't see us. "Do you trust me?"

God, he wants an answer that I don't have. "I trust you with this," I finally say, and he nods, as if he already knew the answer. But when my eyes catch his, I see a turbulent midnight there. He thinks this is our goodbye fuck, this is some final gift he doesn't deserve but can't keep himself from taking.

I don't want it to be our goodbye fuck. I don't want that at all. But before I can tell him this, his big hands are in my panties, finding my wet place and penetrating me without warning.

I gasp and arch against him, the small bite of pain heavenly against the pleasure, like salt on chocolate. But that's nothing compared to what happens to him. As my body clasps his fingers, he gives a fierce growl against my neck, like an animal that's just scented his mate, and suddenly he's yanking my panties down and tearing at his belt.

"Need inside," he grunts.

"God, yes, fucking *yes*, do it, do it—"

He frees his cock and I nearly expire at the sight of it. It's thick and straight and a yummy dusky color, and it wedges its way through his opened trousers like a weapon. Like a scepter. Ready to ruin me and rule me.

I can't wait. Like literally can't wait. I'm arching and mewing against him like a fussy kitten.

He reaches for his pocket and his head snaps up. "I don't have a condom."

For a moment, I'm speechless—Church *always* had condoms because I always needed fucking, and usually more than once—but then I let out a giggle that echoes around the exhibit.

His broken-soft smile returns, although his eyes are still wild animal eyes. "What, Miss Tenpenny?"

"Just—" I cradle his jaw with my hand. "If I hadn't believed you weren't planning on being forgiven before, I believe it now. Because if you thought there was any chance of this happening, I know you would have had like twenty condoms in your wallet."

He shakes his head, then presses his lips to my palm. "What have I told you about hyperbole? It's beneath your intellect. Naturally, I would've only put ten condoms in there."

I laugh again and he bites my palm.

"I have an IUD now," I tell him, my laughter edging back into fervent need. "And I'm clean. Church, if you mean it, if you meant what you said about not being with anyone since me—"

"I meant it. You want me inside you now? Bare?"

His words are hungry, and that hunger stirs me past enduring. I've never had him like this, raw and intimate. Just Church. Primal, naked Church.

"Please," I beg, pushing my hips forward. My panties are down far enough that I kick them to one side and I use a hand to hold up my dress so he can see the place I need filled. I don't want there to be any mistaking what's his to take. What's his to ease himself with.

Church gives a low groan and his erection surges, growing even thicker, the skin pulling taut and shiny. "I need to fuck you," he says, somehow both coldly and hoarsely in that contradictory way of his.

"Please take it, God, just *please,*" I whine, reaching for him, but he stops my hands by grabbing my wrists and pinning them above my head with one hand as he gives the room a quick search.

Then he takes himself in a big hand and notches himself right at my pussy. I wrap a leg around his waist to open myself up to him, and the action spreads my flesh open so that now the searing heat of his crown is pushed right against where I'm wettest.

A hollow groan escapes his throat, and his head drops down between his shoulders, as if even this small contact is too much to bear. For a moment, we just breathe and shiver like this, with his head ducked and his cock spreading me open and his hips poised to thrust.

"Church," I breathe.

"I know," he breathes back. "I'm just—*fuck,* I need it, but I also need a moment to be grateful for this, Charlotte, because I am grateful. So fucking grateful. Just a moment more, just be patient a moment more for me."

Grateful.

His gratitude guts me. I'm slain by it, and I'll be slain every time I think of it for the rest of my life, but even in broken gratitude, Church keeps my hands pinned, and when his head lifts, his expression is my favorite one in the world. The one of a god with a sacrifice to devour.

"Now for the rest," he says arrogantly, but also reverently, and pushes up into me. Just the head, no more than an inch, but already I feel pierced by him, invaded and spread. I'm wet—wetter than I've ever been maybe—but Church's cock is no laughing matter. He gives me another fat inch, and I suck in a breath, writhing on it.

It aches. It feels perfect.

It aches.

It feels perfect.

"Problem?" he murmurs, giving me even more and splitting me in two in the process.

My head hits the case behind me. "I . . . forgot."

The corner of his sharp mouth curves—not his soft smile from earlier, but that familiar cruel one I love so much. "Forgot what, Charlotte? How hard this cock gets for you?"

Another shove, another inch—and another gasp pinched out of me.

"How deep I go? Or how much your sweet body has to work to take me?"

He's only about halfway in, and everything below my navel feels like it's being squeezed in a massive fist. I'm panting, rolling my head along the case wall behind me, and he slides a hand between my thigh and his waist and then pushes me open. He pulls back a few inches and slides back in, my body letting him go deeper this time.

He lets out a very male, very satisfied grunt. "Good girl."

I look down to where we're joined and moan. The hard flesh spearing me is straight from mythology—or maybe pornography. Maybe both. "You're a giant," I manage. "Or some kind of mutant, maybe."

"Sorry," he says, forcing his way deeper and making my eyes flutter in the process.

"You don't sound sorry," I manage.

"I'm not," he says.

"Asshole."

One of his dark eyebrows lifts in amusement. "What should I say, Charlotte? It's terrible to see you flushed and panting as you try to take my cock? I hate feeling you squeezed so tight around me that I can barely move? Sorry my penis is so big?"

"It would be a start," I mumble.

Church looks down then to see what I just saw—the place where his velvet-smooth organ breaches me, and his jaw tics. His grip tightens on my wrists and thigh, as he seems to struggle with some powerful urge.

I know what it is.

"Take it," I say. There's no brattiness in my voice just now, and no legitimate anger. There's no hurt, and no blame. There's only the love for him that five years ago fell on me like a curse, in this very room. The love that was born to be offered and then taken. A love for temples and secret sacrifices in the dark.

His head snaps up and his eyes meet mine and they're pure, liquid midnight. And then I'm impaled on him, lanced all the way up to my heart.

There's pressure and heat and an urgent tightness

twisting into something too unformed to be called pleasure. The raw place where pain met bliss was Church's favorite place to keep me, and he didn't need ropes or floggers to do it. Just his long, perfect body. Just his huge hands pinning me still and forcing me open for his erection.

I have to bite my lip to keep myself from coming right then and there.

"Little supplicant," he breathes and then his forehead rests against mine as we pant and tremble together. "You feel—fuck—how will I live without the way you feel? The way you shiver against me when you're getting close? The way you bite at that freckled lip? How?"

I part my lips to say something—I'm not sure what, but something about how I don't want him to live without it either—and he kisses me with a sudden fierceness that steals my breath and my words.

I can taste gratitude all over his kiss, and when I lick it off his tongue, when I search out more from inside his mouth, his grip on me turns punishing. Below our kiss, he starts the fucking, moving in shallow, grinding thrusts that have an orgasm burning bright and hot behind my clit, and I'm going to come already, I'm going to come after only a few seconds with my Church inside me—

I look down again, unable to resist the carnal mechanics of it all, the animal sight of it.

"Do it," Church orders. "Give me what's mine."

I break apart for him, on him, around him. I can't see and I can't hear—I can only feel and thrash and cry his name as my pussy clenches and releases in abrupt, shuddering waves. It's all hot, mindless sensation, and it's flowing everywhere in my body, from my seizing lower belly down to the soles of my feet and the aching beads of my nipples. Everything feels and aches and unravels for my Church, and he knows it, he knows it's all for him, that my pleasure is his, my pain is his, that *I* am his. He may think I'm only his right here in this moment, he may think that he'll never get to own me again after this, but that doesn't erase the totality of his possession. Of his need to brand me inside and out.

As my body wrings itself out with release, Church seems to lose all patience. All control. My wrists are dropped so he can shove my dress up even higher and squeeze my breast; my thigh is pressed against the case so that my cunt is completely open for his needs. His inhales come in rasping snarls and his exhales in short, angry growls.

And his fucking—his fucking is unstoppable. A cruel weapon meant to command me, and my pulsing sex is evidence that he already does. Not that he seems satisfied with a single orgasm from me. No, he won't be satisfied until I'm wrecked, until I can barely stand and his fuck is the only thing keeping me upright.

"Give me more," he whispers in my ear. "Give me everything until it's all mine."

I can't speak, I can't hardly breathe—this was how it used to be between us, this is what I've been secretly keening for: this ravenous hunger he had for me, like he'll die if he doesn't swallow me whole.

And it turns out that in order to live, I need to be eaten alive.

What a lewd picture we make. Anyone walking in could see this cold, dangerous boy with his belt dangling around his hips, his angry cock buried inside a squirming girl with her dress shoved up to her waist and her cheeks flushed from his dirty, filthy attentions.

Anyone could see this for what it is—a liturgy as frantic as it is holy. A sacrifice being taken.

I come again.

Now, it is really only him keeping me pinned against the wall, and as he grinds into me with that massive thing, I slowly melt against him. My hands paw limply at his biceps as my head drops onto his shoulder and lolls there, like a doll's. And he fucks me like a doll, like a plaything.

"You were right," I tell him, the words husky and air-starved from all the orgasms. "You are still my temple."

"And you are my prayer," he growls back. "*Mine.*"

Underneath my fingertips and against my stomach and between his legs, all of him goes impossibly taut, impossibly hard. Even as one part of him surges into me, the rest of him trembles and shakes and shivers, like he's got a fever. Like he's sick with needing to come.

And then he does.

His eyelids lower, his jaw flexes, and every single muscle in his body seems intent on pushing in deeper, on pumping into me harder, and right when he gives a thrust so fierce I feel my foot lift off the floor, he gives a darkly erotic growl, and releases into me with long, heavy pulses.

He keeps me pinned as he fills me, and it's all so wet, so dirty, to feel him like this without a condom, and I love it, I want more of it, I want it all the time.

He stabs into me again and again, using his own spend to make the slides slick and fast as he chases the last clenches of his pleasure and makes sure he leaves every last drop between my legs. But for as carnal and raw as it all is below, his hands are grabbing and grabbing above, like he can't get me close enough. Like I'll never be close enough to his heart.

We're sweating, indecent, and still so very exposed, but I never want to move. I just want to curl into his strong chest forever.

I feel his lips on my hair, and then his nose as he breathes me in.

"Charlotte," he says miserably. "My sweet, brilliant Charlotte."

"Church, I—"

"You don't have to tell me," he says, pressing his lips to my temple and then easing free of my body. "I know."

I huff. "I don't think you do."

He doesn't respond to me with anything other than a nod of resignation. He thinks I'm about to tell him to go to hell, and he would go there meekly if I did. *Meekly*.

My Church, meek and mortal, and all because he thinks he deserves the worst. I mean, he does, but it's also not the point right now.

The point is that I don't want to tell him to go to hell. I don't want him to go away. I don't want him going anywhere except everywhere I'm going.

He kneels to tug my dress down and help me step into my panties. "Will you listen to me?" I ask.

"Of course," he says.

"I love you," I say and then my breath gets all stuttery and short, because suddenly nothing feels as important as getting this right. "I love you and I don't want you to stay away from me. I want you close. I want you next to me, inside me. I want to belong to you again."

He's looking up from where he kneels at my feet, and I see a thousand expressions passing over his face. Shock and then hope and then guarded concern. "We just fucked, Charlotte. I don't think it's the right time for you to make concessions—"

"They're not concessions," I say. I run a fingertip over the scar on his cheek and then trail my fingers down to his jaw so I can keep his face lifted to mine. "They're what I want."

"But I fucked up," he says hoarsely. "You shouldn't want them."

"Maybe," I say, using my other hand to brush the dark hair away from his forehead. "But I do. So."

My words do nothing to ease the turmoil in his expression, and he closes his eyes, as if he can't look at me while he says what he says next because otherwise he won't have the strength to say it. "Charlotte, please. Please don't compromise on this. Don't compromise for me."

I don't spare him the truth. "I'm not," I tell him bluntly. "I don't trust you right now and I can't tell you that tomorrow will be the same as today. I definitely can't promise you that I'll ever put on a wedding dress for you again."

His eyes open at this, full of shame, and I hate that my proud Church is willing to look my blame in the face but not my love.

"I don't have answers to a lot of questions about us," I admit, and I think of the four-years-ago Charlotte, trying not to cry on the Tube while people politely ignored the way her dress spilled over their feet. I won't betray that Charlotte by unequivocally forgiving what was done to her. But I also can't betray the Charlotte I am today—the one who is desperately in love with the possessive, hungry mystery that is James Cason. "But when I ask myself, *what do I want today*, I know the answer to that. I want you. I want to see if I can find all those other answers in your arms. I want that more than anything."

His sapphire eyes search mine. "Are you sure, Charlotte?"

I take a deep breath. It feels good to admit this, it feels so good to set down resentment to reach for something sweeter. "Today, Church. Today, I'm sure."

He gets slowly to his feet, setting his clothes to rights

without ever taking his eyes from mine. Once he's completely dressed again, he puts his hand over my heart, like he owns it.

"This is mine again?" he asks in a low, shaking voice. There's fear there, and awe, and hope. Trembling, eager hope.

"Today, Church. And you can ask me again tomorrow."

He leans and catches my mouth with his—a brushing, stirring kiss that promises wicked, greedy things. "Then I better make today count."

And in true Church fashion, he tugs me impatiently out of the exhibit and down the stairs. He tugs me all the way to his house—and once the estate agent is booted from the premises and my brother knows I'll be out late—we finally do what we want most in the world to do.

We worship.

EPILOGUE

Church

"I don't want to go home," Charlotte says with a sigh. In front of her, the Mediterranean sparkles blue and brilliant, and a warm Tel Aviv breeze toys with her curls, occasionally revealing flashes of her delightfully freckled neck.

"I'll bring you back," I say, coming to join her on the balcony. "You'll need to have more experience out here if you want to curate Levantine collections anyway."

She pouts a little, that freckled lower lip making a plump little curve. "Do we really have to go back to Oxford?"

"We do," I tell her, wrapping her in my arms and pulling her so her back rests against my chest. We look out at the turquoise sea together while I nuzzle against her hair. She smells like sunshine and shampoo—when we got back to Tel Aviv and a real hotel after four weeks digging near a dusty tell, she went straight for the shower and scrubbed her hair for about forty minutes. "But I'll take you to that standing stone you like and fuck you for hours next to it. Will that scratch your prehistory itch?"

"It's not the same," she fusses, but she does push her bottom against my lap. "But you can still fuck me for hours. That part's okay."

"Hmm. How about we start on it now?"

"But we're supposed to go to dinner with—"

I'm already slinging her over my shoulder and taking her back to the bed. I give her backside a swat before throwing her on the bed and then crawling over her. "Legs open, little supplicant. Show me what I want."

I'm barely patient enough to wait for her to obey, wanting to tear her dress off with my teeth and then spear her with my neglected cock. Having Charlotte on a dig with me again was profoundly wonderful—I loved seeing her face as she finally freed some tiny, broken treasure from the earth, and I savored having her thoughts and observations available to me in the field. But it was also a problem, because all of the things that made it fulfilling also made me fucking horny. And turns out it's next to impossible to get a leg over in the middle of the desert, so I've been very, very deprived.

Since that day three years ago in the museum, it feels like everything and nothing has changed. I rented a modest flat in London and stayed close to Charlotte while Jax finished school. Charlotte refused to move in with me—but she did finally accept my gift of rent that first year, which meant she could quit catering and sign up for night classes at UCL. She graduated—with honors—at the same time Jax did. And now she's pursuing her graduate degree at Oxford, where I've also taken a post. Apparently my reputation was good enough to withstand my abrupt departure from UCL, and since we both came to Oxford at the same time, it was easy to prevent any nepotist speculation from the get-go.

Besides, I'm only at Oxford because she's there. Once she wants to leave, I'll follow her to wherever she finds the job of her dreams. She's my passion now, and my calling.

Three years ago, Charlotte said five fateful words to me. *Today, the answer is yes*. And I've spent every day since then asking her, as gently and patiently as a monster like me is able, *what about today?*

Every day, in a blessing I don't understand or deserve, the answer has been the same as it was on the first.

Charlotte pulls up her dress and spreads her thighs and I feel as thunderstruck by the sight as I did the first time I saw it seven years ago. Without bothering to do anything else, I pull my linen pants down to expose my aching erection and then push it against where she's wet. I love this part, when I can just begin to feel the tight grip of her, because it means I'm about to be as close to her as I possibly can. It means that, at least for a while, I'll be able to make her feel as breathless and split open as she makes me.

"I forgot to ask this morning," I say as I jab forward. Her back arches deliciously and I lean down to bite at my favorite freckle. "What about today?"

I expect her to give her usual answer, and so I'm already stroking my cock into her pussy, ready to segue to the part of the fucking where she's too well-pleasured for conversation, when she says, "Today, the answer is forever."

My body gets the message before my mind can process it, and I go still, looking down at her. "What?" I ask blankly.

Her mouth twitches in a small smile that's smug, and a little nervous. She reaches into the pocket of her dress, and I feel her slim fingers brushing against my hip as she searches.

And then she pulls out a ring.

It's a silky, matte gold, finely—but still visibly—beaten, with the small hammer marks making angles and faces all around the band.

"I made it," she says shyly. "There's a local blacksmith who helped. I couldn't find a ring antique enough to be interesting to us, so I thought I'd fashion it myself."

"Charlotte," I say, trying to be careful, but failing, failing. My heart is massive, huge, it's taking up my entire body—except, of course, the part still nestled in Charlotte's snug warmth. That part just continues to throb happily. "What is this?"

"It's an engagement ring," she says. "Will you marry me?"

I can barely think over my giant, bloody heart. "Do you—are you very sure, little one? Because I don't need this. I'll live the rest of my life as the happiest man alive even if we're still taking it day by day."

She shakes her head on the pillow, gray eyes clear but serious. "I don't want that. I needed time to trust you again—and trust myself. I needed space to see my promises to myself and my brother through. I needed to make sure that if I forgave you, I was doing it for the right reasons. But the past three years have given me that. And I want more. I want everything."

"I do owe you everything."

"You do."

"I don't deserve to give it you."

She pulls one lovely shoulder up to her ear in the laying-down version of a shrug. "I'm ready for you to deserve it."

I didn't think my heart could get any bigger, but here it is, bigger than me, big enough to hold her inside it. "Charlotte . . ."

She smiles up at me. "What about your answer, my Church? What about today?"

I take in a long breath that's full of her and our sex and the sparkling Tel Aviv evening. If she's ready for me to deserve it, then I shall, and I'll give her everything in return. "Today, the answer is forever," I tell her.

Her smile is so big, it could light up all of Tel Aviv. She reaches for my hand, and soon I have her ring on it. I can barely take my eyes off it, but I do, because nothing is ever as beautiful as my sunny little supplicant.

Tears burn behind my eyes as I scoop my arms underneath her and begin thrusting into my perfect girl, and I murmur everything into her hair as I strum orgasms out of her like music from a harp. I murmur every last word about how gorgeous she is, how clever, how blessed I am, how wrecked she makes me, how I'll never, ever abandon her again. And when I finally come with the sea rushing outside and her ring glinting on my hand, I'm not an angry god or a cold temple.

I am *her* supplicant.

And I will worship at her feet forever.

The end.

Want more broody British heroes and their delicious dirtiness?

Come to Thornchapel, where secrets, heartbreak, and desire send innocent librarian Poe Markham crashing into the gorgeously gothic world of the possessive Auden Guest...

SIERRA SIMONE

Check out A Lesson in Thorns now!

ALSO BY SIERRA SIMONE

Co-Written with Julie Murphy:

A Merry Little Meet Cute (coming October 2022)

The Priest Series:

Priest

Midnight Mass: A Priest Novella

Sinner

Saint

Thornchapel:

A Lesson in Thorns

Feast of Sparks

Harvest of Sighs

Door of Bruises

Misadventures:

Misadventures with a Professor

Misadventures of a Curvy Girl

Misadventures in Blue

The New Camelot Trilogy:

American Queen

American Prince

American King

The Moon (Merlin's Novella)

American Squire (A Thornchapel and New Camelot Crossover)

Co-Written with Laurelin Paige

Porn Star

Hot Cop

The Markham Hall Series:

The Awakening of Ivy Leavold

The Education of Ivy Leavold

The Punishment of Ivy Leavold

The London Lovers:

The Seduction of Molly O'Flaherty

The Wedding of Molly O'Flaherty

ABOUT THE AUTHOR

Sierra Simone is a USA Today bestselling former librarian who spent too much time reading romance novels at the information desk. She lives with her husband and family in Kansas City.

Sign up for her newsletter to be notified of releases, books going on sale, events, and other news!

www.thesierrasimone.com
thesierrasimone@gmail.com

CPSIA information can be obtained
at www.ICGtesting.com
Printed in the USA
BVHW031934250523
664863BV00014B/486

9 781949 364231